D1083189

5   23
STRAND PRICE
5 00

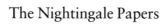

The Nightingale Papers

The Nightingale Papers

David Nokes

ET REMOTISSIMA PROPE

Published by Hesperus Press Limited
4 Rickett Street, London sw6 1ru
www.hesperuspress.com

The Nightingale Papers © David Nokes, 2005
David Nokes asserts his moral right to be identified as the author of this
work under the Copyright, Designs and Patents Act 1988.
First published by Hesperus Press Limited, 2005

Designed and typeset by Fraser Muggeridge
Printed in Jordan by Jordan National Press

ISBN: 1-84391-703-3

All rights reserved. This book is sold subject to the condition that it shall
not be resold, lent, hired out or otherwise circulated without the express
prior consent of the publisher.

For Marie

I

Gillian ran up the stairs into the bedroom, slamming the door behind her. She knelt down beside the unmade bed, lugged out her empty suitcase and threw it on the duvet.

'Come on, Gill. Come down here. Let's talk about it.'

Danny's voice came wafting up the stairwell like an insidious smell. Not a bad smell, exactly; there would be many women who would quite take to it, she thought, packing in the oddments she would need for a couple of days.

'Gill?'

Even she had quite taken to it once. It was louder now; his lecturer's voice, addressing her as if she were a roomful of First Years. Which she had been once, though not a roomful and, thankfully, not one of his. If she had been, this whole affair might well have been avoided. She heard his footsteps on the stairs, the handle turned and the bedroom door was thrown open.

'What are you doing?'

Ignoring him she pulled open a wardrobe drawer, took out a load of bras and knickers and threw them in the suitcase.

'I asked you a question.' He put out a hand to grab her arm but she shook him off.

'Isn't it obvious?'

She tried to flatten down the mound of under-clothes but washing had made them resistant.

'No,' he said, 'it isn't.' Bending down to catch a pair of knickers from falling to the floor their foreheads clashed.

'Sorry,' she said, then cursed herself. He smiled, rubbing his forehead, holding out the blue embroidered panties.

'Weren't these the ones you wore – or rather didn't – that time in Nice when...'

'I haven't a clue,' she threw them angrily in the suitcase.

'I'm sure they were, you know, because...'

'No doubt you're right. You always are.' She made shooing gestures with her hands.

'What?' he said, ignoring them. She had an image of him putting down a very large anchor on the end of a very long chain.

'I have things to do.' She put out her hands to push him away but he held them and pulled her close.

'Not yet,' he said. 'First you have to explain what all this is about.'

'I should've thought that was obvious,' she said, wriggling her arms in a way he found exhilarating. 'Let go.'

'Not to me it isn't,' he said as she twisted to get free. 'You're not still fretting about Carstairs? Is that it?'

'Leave me alone,' she said. He began to smile. 'Oh come on. That was just a bit of fun.'

'To you,' she said.

'To everyone.'

'To Carstairs?'

Danny grinned. 'Maybe not initially. But, I'm sure when he thinks about it...'

'Oh yeah. Like you.'

'No,' admitted Danny, 'not quite like me.'

'No,' said Gill, 'thank God.'

What had begun as a lunchtime conversation had become, at least in Gillian's eyes, rather more significant. She was a freelance illustrator whose main source of income, for the past three or four years, had been children's books; her clients, though few in number, were delighted by her sense of colour and confidence of line. A year ago she'd been offered an exhibition in an upstairs gallery off Chiswick Mall. She almost died of fright and from the start was talking the whole thing down. Danny heard her on the phone telling people that of course it wasn't Bond Street or Chelsea, just a sort of attic place in Chiswick which, without an A–Z, would be very hard to find. She managed to make it sound about as exciting as a jumble sale for Oxfam, he'd told her.

She picked up the suitcase and hurried down the stairs before there was the chance of further interruption.

'You're coming back?' For the first time there was an edge of something less comic in his tone. The door slammed, and there were sounds, like Clive Hancock on the morning after a party, of her elderly Volkswagen coughing into life, and spluttering away.

Hancock had begun the unpleasantness by suggesting a small painting Jim Baxter had acquired that morning, at a car-boot sale at Reading, was only worth 'a tenner'.

'Which is stretching it,' he said, turning it this way and that. 'What is it, anyway?'

Baxter rescued the picture from his hands and said the rural scene was mid-nineteenth-century, at least according to the dealer, which seemed accurate enough. There were hills, a tiny cave, some overhanging trees, a cow and a stream.

'Amazing what you can pick up,' he said.

'If you're not very careful,' quipped Hancock. The witticism had no effect on Baxter, whose enthusiasm was unquenchable. He'd had to haggle with the dealer, who had been asking three hundred for it, 'but I beat him down and beat him down.'

He beamed and no one spoke. Jim Baxter was small, pink and utterly cherubic; the idea of him beating anybody down was wonderfully implausible.

'In the end he let me have it for two-forty. I mean, for the frame alone...'

Hancock conceded, with a smile, that the frame was worth a bob or two. Hugo Carstairs, who had spent most of dinner studying the frayed ends of his shirt-cuffs, raised his head.

'For what it's worth –' he said, 'which I know is not a lot – I love it. So understated and so very English. I have to say' – he said to Baxter – 'that I am deeply envious.'

He leant forward, cradling the painting awkwardly between his palms, sticking his jaw out and leaning his head to one side in a way both aggressive and diffident. 'A little gem,' he murmured.

A little later, after quite a lot of claret, Hancock returned to the painting and said to his mind the thing was definitely pastiche. 'Pseudo-nineteenth-century pastiche' was what he actually said, as though doing his best to be complimentary to Baxter. Hugo said again how much he liked it and Hancock couldn't resist saying that 'it didn't surprise him in the least'. Whether he would have said it had it not been for the claret, is anybody's guess. There was a pause, then Hugo, speaking rather slowly and softly, said he'd seen far worse things for sale in Bond Street. At all sorts of Bond Street prices. Baxter wondered about contacting Sotheby's for an opinion but Hugo was rather discouraging. Of course, he said, he could. And no doubt – for a fee – they would offer their opinion. But so what? Why was everybody so obsessed by money? The painting was glorious. Leave it at that – he sighed and had another sliver of Camembert.

'Ask Teddy,' said Hancock, pouring the last of the claret into his glass, 'get him to take a dekko. Should be simple enough. Get him to give it the Fenton seal of approval: an early Cotman, a middle period Crome.'

'I'll pretend I didn't hear that,' said Carstairs.

'Happens all the time,' said Hancock, drinking down the claret; at which point Gillian offered more cheese, sensing civilised conversation was losing out to something darker.

'It's a racket,' said Hancock, 'a bloody good racket. The only sensible art criticism these days is in the Wall Street Journal. The rest of it, quite frankly, is just pretentious bullshit.'

Hugo sat at the end of the table, fidgeted with the final parings of his Camembert and silently concluded that Hancock's opinions were designed to goad him. Staring hard at the cloth he ventured to doubt that 'even Clive' could be so philistine as to suggest a relationship between artistic values and those which applied in the market.

'You don't know him,' whispered Baxter's wife, Sandie.

'Ah, but you see,' said Hugo, wearily, 'I do.'

Hancock made a speech, on behalf, as he put it, of 'philistines everywhere'. If the market didn't decide on artistic values, who did? Some snobby little clique of *connoisseurs?* – It was remarkable the venom he could inject into a single word. He was a fine one to call other people snobs, said Baxter with sudden ferocity, blushing bright pink. He immediately apologised and everyone, especially his wife, told him not to be so silly; but it was rather splendid to see what a furious Jim Baxter would be like.

'Actually,' said Hancock calmly, 'I wasn't calling anyone a snob.'

Baxter apologised again, blushed fiercely and, in his nervousness, dropped the picture. Which would have been the end of it, had not Danny, leaning down to retrieve it from the floor, remarked that if it came to that, he 'would rather be a snob than a hypocrite'. Some of Hugo's celery seemed to stick in his throat; he had a sort of choking fit and Gillian gave him water to drink, but his hand shook so a good half of it spilt down his trousers. She looked fiercely at Danny and mouthed to him to leave it; but he didn't. What he couldn't stand – he said, opening a Budweiser (the claret being all gone) – were moral snobs; the kind who called their snobbery Art, with a capital 'A', and expected the public to pay for it. Hugo ceased his coughing fit, sipped his water and dabbed his trousers with a paper tissue.

'That painting, for example,' said Hancock, 'you could pass off that painting anywhere.'

'Anywhere,' Danny agreed.

'It's just a racket.'

Hugo, looking more saddened than horrified, cleared his throat.

Luckily, though no great admirer of the art trade – he said, speaking slowly and with deliberation – he was sufficiently convinced, on reliable evidence, that the whole matter was conducted on a more reputable basis than they pretended. For example – he took some more water – there was the whole matter of provenance.

'Easy,' said Danny, breaking in on him. A couple of letters was all it needed.

'You could probably get away with one,' said Hancock.

'Dated sometime around the turn of the century. Some estate papers, or the records of some provincial art-dealer that had died or gone out of business.'

'But the picture itself,' said Carstairs, rather disturbed and not a little hurt by this sudden onslaught, 'is a very fine picture. Not a Crome, perhaps. No,' he picked it up and looked at it, 'certainly not a Crome.' As it happened – he handed the picture back to Baxter – he knew his Crome rather well, being brought up in the Wolds.

Possibly so – said Danny – possibly he was right to say it wasn't Crome. But Cotman? Those ochres and umbers, they were very Cotman.

Carstairs was unconvinced. He claimed to know his Cotman quite as well, if not better than, his Crome. There were a hundred tiny differences any expert would immediately see.

'Such as?' Danny begged the painting back and pointed out the heavy but luminous sky, abundant hollyhocks and thick clumps of thatch. If anyone had told him the painting was a Cotman, he'd have believed them. No question about it. He paused and 'thought' for a moment.

There was one it particularly reminded him of, he said; in the Barber Institute. What was it called? Hugo must know it. Quite famous. Scarborough something? No, Bridlington. Now he remembered, Bridlington Bay. Hugo must know it. Famous one. Hugo wasn't at all sure. He vaguely thought he might know the one Danny had in mind, but he wasn't at all sure.

'Famous one,' said Danny. 'Ruskin commented on it. What was it? Something about it "breathing the authentic spirit of provincial England."'

'Ah yes,' said Hugo, for whom Ruskin was a particular favourite.

'Or was it native? The native spirit, or the authentic spirit?'

Hugo said he thought native sounded rather more *authentic*, and could not restrain a smirk at his little witticism.

'I could look it up.'

'No, no. There's no need for that.'

'It's no trouble…' Danny stood up.

'No, no,' said Hugo.

He remembered the comment?

Hugo nodded.

And the picture too. He remembered the picture?

'Vividly,' he said, 'in the Barber Institute.'

Danny sat back in his chair and folded his arms across his chest. 'That's funny…' he said. 'I just made the whole thing up.'

Moving out had been on Gillian's mind for weeks, and the Cotman incident gave her the perfect excuse. It wasn't that she had suddenly ceased to love Danny; but, over the years (they had been together almost four) something had altered. He now seemed rarely to notice her and she couldn't remember when they had last been out together. Whether this was 'it', she couldn't say. She wanted time on her own, to think;

when Alice asked her to water plants while she went off to Greece, it seemed the perfect opportunity.

She went to college early the next day and knocked on Carstairs' door. She had been upset by the incident of the painting and intended to let him know she had nothing to do with it. He affected to have forgotten the whole business, but she guessed that was a ruse. She said she hoped very much he wouldn't bear a grudge.

'A grudge?' He turned and smiled his world-weary smile at her; why ever should he bear a grudge? 'I was wrong and he was right. My own stupid fault.' He went to his cupboard and poured two glasses of his driest, finest sherry.

'You're very kind.'

The room was cluttered with books; they were piled high on chairs, on the floor, double-stacked along the shelves and window ledges.

'It's what the middle-aged are reduced to,' he replied.

'I'm sure you're always kind.'

It crossed Hugo's mind, for a moment, to attempt to seduce this woman who had made a special trip to him to apologise. That would pay the little bastard back. Unless, of course, this was another of his tricks.

'Oh I do hope not,' he said.

'But the way he did it! I tell you, honestly, I had no idea.'

No, this was not a game, he thought – or else Gillian was a very inexpert player. She meant every word she was saying.

'Ah yes,' he said, 'the technique! It's easy to see, my dear, that you are not an academic. I hate to disabuse you, but really, it wasn't such a master-stroke. I was a fool. I made the mistake of bluffing...' he sipped his sherry, 'fatal, I'm afraid. It's a game, much affected by research students.' He searched along his bookshelves, took down a fat ring-bound file with navy covers and flicked it open midway through. It was the draft of someone's thesis. 'See, here,' he said, pushing the file across the desk towards her and pointing to the bottom of the page, 'that footnote. The date, 1776 – that's wrong. There's no such edition. The third edition is 1771, but that doesn't have the reading he requires. The fourth edition does, but doesn't appear till 1784.' He sat back.

'It's a mistake,' said Gillian.

'I doubt it,' said Hugo, shaking his head. 'I doubt it very much. Such a mistake would be quite difficult to contrive by error. No, I fear it's a trap, designed to catch me out and show either that I don't know my editions, or that I haven't read the footnotes.'

'What will you do?'

'Do? Why, nothing.'

'Nothing?'

'And spoil the student's triumph? Writing a thesis is a thankless business at the best of times. I think it would be churlish to deprive him of his little victory. More sherry?'

A flight of pigeons wheeled around Somerset House and came to rest above the windows of St Mary-le-Strand. Gillian put down her glass, a little flushed, and leant forward.

'But if the lecturer knows this?...'

Hugo's eyes shone. 'Go on,' he said.

'Suppose he, the lecturer, were saying things that...' she paused, 'weren't true.'

'Naming no names,' he beamed.

'But, just suppose for a moment...'

'Put the case, as Jaggers says. Wonderful character that Jaggers...'

'He were saying things which were... deliberate untruths...'

Carstairs pursed his lips. 'Very tricky ground we're stepping onto here. To say what's untrue necessarily implies a clear knowledge of what's true; not a private conviction but a general consensus.' He shook his head. 'Very tricky,' he said.

'But say he...'

'Naming no names.'

'No, all right, naming no names. Say he said, oh, I don't know, say he said Shakespeare was born in 1800 at Wigan...'

'An unfortunate example,' said Carstairs, whose eyes still beamed. 'There's considerable critical opinion, including that of the present holder of the Percy Chair, which argues that Shakespeare,' he made little speech-marks in the air, 'is a nineteenth-century invention. Not the bones of course, they don't mean the skeleton at Stratford, but the body of his works.' He turned suddenly to Gillian and asked if she had read a book called *Shakespeare our Contemporary* by Jan Kott? Gillian shook her head.

'You should,' he said, 'explains a lot.' He turned to his shelves and reached down a well-thumbed copy – full of perfect gems. '"I'll put a girdle round about the earth / In forty minutes"; Shakespeare was not far wrong. The first Russian sputnik encircled the earth in forty-seven minutes.' He shut the book and re-shelved it. 'No,' he said, 'I'd be hard pressed to spot a *lie*. Not really a critical concept, lying.'

'But just suppose –'

'Put the case,' he interrupted; 'helps me to concentrate.'

'Put the case,' said Gill, 'that someone tried to fake a document. A manuscript...'

'Oh, this is interesting,' said Hugo. 'An original, like Chatterton? Or a pastiche, like a fifth book of the *Dunciad*?'

'No, I mean actually faking an original literary manuscript.'

'Well,' said Carstairs, thinking as he said it, 'they would have to be very clever and up to all the modern checks on paper, ink, stuff like that. And I don't know anything about the legal position. Legally, I'm sure the whole thing would be pretty fraught. The prices these things fetch! There was a sale at Sotheby's just last month, some notebooks of Trelawny's, just jottings, nothing more. You wouldn't believe the prices. But from a purely critical point of view?'

Gillian nodded.

'Well,' he paused. 'I have to say I don't know.'

Gillian looked distinctly depressed but Hugo shrugged. 'To a non-professional I realise that may appear rather vague,' Gillian tried to make no comment, 'but this thing, if it were ever to happen, would be wrapped in all kinds of duplicity which might raise the "forgery" to a state of interest for itself.'

He turned back to his bookshelves, searched past the stacks of paperbacks to some handsome mock-leather bindings, removed a book and showed it to her. The spine said *The Double Falshood* by William Shakespeare.

'Know it?' he asked, and Gillian shook her head.

'I'm not surprised,' he said. 'No one does. The play turned up mysteriously in the eighteenth century, discovered by Lewis Theobald, Pope's chief dunce in the *Dunciad*. Pope and Theobald were both editing Shakespeare...'

'Who wasn't invented till the nineteenth century?'

Hugo smiled broadly. 'You get the idea,' he said. 'Theobald claimed to have three copies of this play, by Shakespeare. The only trouble was that, according to him, they weren't very good. So he thought the best thing was to tidy them up prior to publication. So...' He opened up the title page of the volume and Gillian read:

'*The Double Falshood*, A tragedy, by Lewis Theobald and William Shakespeare. What happened to the manuscripts?'

'Good question. They just mysteriously disappeared.'

'If they ever existed!'

Hugo smiled. 'The point is, they never harmed Theobald's reputation at all; on the contrary, he went from strength to strength. You know the death of Falstaff in *Henry V*? "His nose was as sharp as a pen, and a' babbled o' green fields". Good eh? That's Theobald's, not Shakespeare's.'

Gillian turned over the pages of the book, murmuring, 'The Double Falshood…'

'Neat title,' said Carstairs, 'and quite appropriate, really.'

2

The first mention of the Madoc conference appeared the following week, just as Danny was starting to find it rather inconvenient to be alone. For a few days he had revelled in having the house to himself and got drunk every night. By the end of the week, with no message from Gill and no way of getting through to her, he became a little worried. His clothes were in a dirty pile on the bedroom floor, and if she didn't turn up soon he would have to think what to do with them. He tried the numbers of old girlfriends, but every one of them had moved. The Madoc circular came with a little Gothic, pseudo-allegorical logo on the cover, advertising four days in Wales at some sort of Congregationalist College. Danny threw it in the bin. Then the personal letters started arriving from Grant Morris, conference organiser, hoping very much etc. etc. These were personal in form only, being computer-printed with only a hastily scribbled postscript at the end enquiring after Gill (or Jill, as Morris had it). The memo from Carstairs that Danny found shoved under his college door was a different matter. This was a long meandering scrawl on the decline of English studies which, though it did not say so, seemed to imply it was Danny's duty to attend the conference which might otherwise fall prey to *zealots*. He happened across Carstairs in the college gents where he stood, slowly zipping up his fly, leaving a damp crescent-shaped patch down the front of his greenish corduroys, tugging hopelessly at the towel-flo. He made no mention of the Cotman incident, because Carstairs would have forgotten it; a week had passed since then.

'Sorry about the memo thing,' said Carstairs as Danny stood pissing against the stained porcelain. 'Please don't feel under any, you know, obligation. Thing is, I've got myself roped in.' He gave up on the towelflo and waited for Dan to wash his hands.

'Randolph's the star, of course. A propos of which I've been sent a copy of his edition to review. Seen it?'

'As it happens,' said Danny, effortlessly pulling down a length of towelflo, 'I'm reviewing it too.'

'Really?' said Carstairs. 'For somewhere rather grand, I imagine...'

'*The Sunday Globe*.'

Carstairs softly whistled. 'They must pay a packet,' he said. He was doing it for somewhere much humbler. '*Poetry Newsletter*. Ever see it? They don't pay a penny. What do you think of it, by the way, or shouldn't I ask?'

Danny pushed open the door and said he thought it had all sorts of traditional strengths.

'Really,' said Carstairs, inviting him for tea. 'I thought it was pretty crappy.'

Back in his office Hugo viewed the row of plump, damp teabags drying on the radiator, whose preservation sprang not from meanness but a dedication to ritual. The afternoon sun caught his profile as he stood, staring out the window, waiting for the kettle to boil.

'Curious,' he said, 'the way ideas and attitudes you start out with never really go. I suppose,' he said, scooping two of the plumpest teabags into coronation mugs, 'it's an instinct thing. They seem more real. I don't mean they never change. What is it Eliot says?' – steam billowed across the room, misting up the window – '"Sensibility changes from age to age, whether we will or no."'

He wrapped his grubby handkerchief around the kettle handle and poured boiling water into the mugs. 'For me, it was Leavis or Lewis, the critic or the scholar. What battles we had! Departments split right down the middle – the Oxford History or the Pelican Guides! They were the rival paths, the Guermantes or Meseglise way. Take sugar if you want it...' He pointed to a rather battered packet. 'Now that's all ancient history. We're faced with Lacan, Derrida and that woman whose name I can't pronounce which is no doubt terribly significant. Sick-something?'

'Cixous?'

'Is that it?' said Carstairs, whose voice rarely hinted at irony. 'If you want milk I'm afraid I've only got this powdered stuff.' He gestured towards a tin whose lid was wedged on tight with layers of dust. Danny said he would take it black. Carstairs fished out the teabag with the end of a pencil and passed the cup across, replacing the teabag on the radiator. 'It's not that I dislike or disapprove of them particularly,' he said,

'I just don't engage with them. I keep on waiting for the old ideas to return. I suppose that's the classic definition of a reactionary. Don't drink it if it's too awful. I know it's pretty foul but I sort of like it. I know they won't of course. Come back, I mean. Intellectually I fully appreciate the inevitability of historical change. It's just instinctively that I rebel. Here I am, a professor of literature, but what do I profess? Here, give me that if you don't want it. Don't tip it on the plants, it kills them.'

Absent-mindedly he began sipping at the cup he'd taken from Danny's hands.

'Weren't you working on Madoc once?'

'The other Madoc,' said Danny, quickly, 'the father, not the son.'

'Oh,' said Carstairs despondently, then brightened up. 'Still, it doesn't make much difference, does it? If it's a matter of expenses, even these days…' He turned to the window and Danny stood up to go.

'I don't *feel* like a reactionary,' Hugo said, suddenly, 'whatever that feels like. I'm still Labour and so on… still…' he paused, 'I suppose you can't get more conservative than that.' He chuckled, and his breath left a circle, like a wreath, against the window pane.

Danny held two convictions which eased his existence considerably: the first was that his was not an original mind; the second, that the academic business was a game. For example, the week before when Baxter had gone down with flu, Danny happily stood in for him in giving a slide lecture on *The Rake's Progress*. Only afterwards, when the students had all gone home, did he realise that he'd made an error loading the slides into the carousel, and shown them all the wrong way round. But ideologically, as he remarked to Baxter on his return, he viewed it as something of a plus, since it demystified the iconic status of the images, and made the students see them, literally, from a different point of view. Baxter puffed at his pipe and nodded, but next day there was a notice on the Departmental notice-board offering to give the lecture again. Baxter had an original mind and, for him, academic life was a nightmare. When young, Danny had sent sample chapters from his novels to publishers whose comments, veiling damnation behind faint praise ('it was, however, felt...') were always in the passive voice. He made it a principle, from that day forward, to express his opinions actively, and to favour the personal pronoun – I think. He was (in his view) the Descartes of contemporary reviewers.

The McWhinnie review was going badly. These days Danny seldom bothered with academic books, but in McWhinnie's case he decided to make an exception. It was an exception he was now regretting. McWhinnie had been his tutor up at Oxford and even now he still received a card each Christmas signed, in McWhinnie's spidery handwriting, 'Yours ever, Randolph.' Randolph Frazier McWhinnie came late to academic life, belonging to the generation whose formal education was interrupted by war. His record, with the Cameron Highlanders, was highly distinguished; decorated for bravery in Burma and wounded in the Normandy landings. In peacetime he found it hard to settle, finding no equivalent in demob Britain for the exhilaration of being under fire. He tried school-mastering for a spell at a dingy south-coast crammer run by a regimental pal, but the boys, he found, were either louts or duffers. Oxford, when he returned to complete his degree, was much the same – full of pacifists and pinkoes. It made him wonder how in God's name they had ever won the war – or even, in his bleakest moments, why. For McWhinnie the true criterion of poetic greatness was how a poem measured up to gunfire. That was, he said, the acid test. He used to rile his colleagues (pacifists and pinkoes to a man) by recounting how he first read *Tintern Abbey* on the beach at Arromanches, with all about him rockets and mortar fire. His belated undergraduate career was heading for disaster until one afternoon, sitting in Duke Humphry, he stumbled on the delights of bibliography. He had before him two editions of 'The Prelude', the 1805 and the 1850; comparing their two texts he experienced a thrill akin to revelation. It was as if, he said, the whole tract of history marked out by those two dates had been illuminated like a strip of land under the flare path of a raid. In the alteration of adjectives, the transposition of metaphors and rearrangement of lines, McWhinnie identified the cultural scars which separated Trafalgar from the Crimea.

The essay which he subsequently wrote gained him a Fellowship; the book which quickly followed established him as undisputed leader in his field. No one before him had devoted such close attention to the tactical deployment of military metaphors in the works of poets more usually associated with pacific, anti-imperialist attitudes. No one, apart from McWhinnie, possessed sufficient technical familiarity with the lexicon of war to challenge his belligerent theories. Post-McWhinnie it became impossible, for several years, to discuss even the most innocuous of lyrical ballads without a reference to the contemporary state of the anti-Napoleonic arsenal. Mere absence from a poem of specifically bellicose allusions did not in any way compromise the appropriateness of his theories for, as he was wont to assert, hugely pleased to turn the slogans of his Freudian antagonists to his own advantage: 'absence is presence'.

McWhinnie's thesis proved particularly consoling in an era when Britain's military presence in the world was visibly declining. His long-awaited edition of Madoc's *Basque Cantoes* was to be the crowning achievement of his career – yet, unaccountably, the work was plagued by innumerable delays. Commissioned in the early 1970s, it languished for a decade, during which McWhinnie himself suffered several debilitating ailments. At last, promised in a publisher's 1980 catalogue, it reappeared as 'forthcoming' in the subsequent editions for 1981 and 1982, before disappearing entirely in 1983. Rumours circulated concerning the fate of the project: some claimed it was almost finished; others insinuated it had hardly begun. Some claimed to have seen the proofs, while others had it on the best authority that McWhinnie had long since abandoned the whole venture as preposterous. In the intervening years McWhinnie's reputation underwent something of a decline and, from the perspective of the mid-1980s his critical methodology took on a quaint, faintly risible air, a relic of those old pre-Thatcherite days when cultural chauvinism, disguised as liberal values, held sway over linguistic science. When now the work – or part of it – had finally appeared, it seemed less a monument to scholarship than a vestige of some archaic cult. Shrunken and depleted, this First Volume of the *Cantoes*, with no index and only a haphazard, halting Introduction, bore little relation to the fresh confident promise of McWhinnie's early years.

Danny's three years up at Oxford had not been a success. From the start he viewed the place with a suspicion bred from awkwardness. Never one of the cliquey crowd, he affected the status of a loner, dressed entirely in black and carried round volumes of Sartre. His only companions as an undergraduate were uncongenial types who had failed to join, or been excluded from College clubs and drinking parties. Among these, Nevill was the most notable.

He shared tutorials with Nevill during the Hilary Term, after which they drank together – not in the College buttery dominated by OUDS and rowing types, but in a pub down the Cowley Road. Nevill never stopped complaining about Oxford being full of snobs, debs and pseuds, a thread of personal injustice running through all his conversations. He seemed incapable of telling the simplest story without infecting it with rancour, and attracted persecution as a swamp attracts flies.

There was a sense that something persecuted McWhinnie too. In the Oxford of the late 1960s, his military air, his regimental blazer and smatterings of 1940s slang were all faintly comic. Imitations of his mannerisms – the nervous cough before speaking, the concluding 'd'ye see?' the habit of flicking imaginary specks of dust from immaculate blazer sleeves – were a commonplace of College revues. All too often people mistook his fastidiousness for snobbery when, in reality, he was the least snobbish of dons. His punctiliousness was an over-compensation for a deep sense of social unease. There was a precision about his speech which went well beyond the dictates of good taste and succeeded in creating a good deal of conversational alarm among even the most correct of his colleagues. He had nothing queer about him, although – as with most unmarried dons – all kinds of rumours flourished, particularly over the mysterious phone calls he received, when he would blush deep red, go into his inner room, and emerge offering profuse apologies. The most conspicuous source of embarrassment for McWhinnie was his mother, a woman of large build and limited refinements who laboured under the misapprehension that her recently acquired brusque tones and dowager manner had the capacity to transform acts of casual rudeness into stylish eccentricities. She was in the habit of descending unannounced upon McWhinnie's tutorials, depositing large shopping bags from the more exclusive stores about the room while pronouncing loudly on the idleness of College servants. She thought nothing of trying out her latest hats and scarves in front of McWhinnie and his grinning undergraduates: 'There now boys,' she would proclaim, 'what d'you think?' She would rattle on about titled friends, patting the boys on the arm and even, on one memorable occasion, running a comb through McWhinnie's hair.

Nevill regarded the whole business of tutorials as a form of elitist persecution, and a schooner of dry sherry was, to him, a symbol of class intimidation. One week, sunk in the first volume of *Clarissa*, Nevill counterfeited flu, and Danny went to the tutorial alone. Inevitably McWhinnie was most impressed by Lovelace's, hence Richardson's, gifts as a tactician. Richardson, he was convinced, would have made a first-rate general. Like Johnson. Had it not struck Danny, he wondered, how precisely the symmetrical forms of Augustan literature – heroic couplets and antitheses – mimicked the battlefield configurations of the age? When the hour was up, McWhinnie promptly closed the book and reached for the sherry decanter, flicking imaginary specks from his lapel. His hand shook as he measured out the glasses.

'Your friend, Nevill,' he said, settling back into his large leather armchair. 'Can't make up my mind whether he's a dark horse or just exceptionally grey. Seems lost in English. Wouldn't sociology be more his sort of thing?' He pretended to admire Nevill's dogged determination to find symbols of revolution in the most urbane works.

'I suppose he's some sort of Marxist?'

Danny said he did not know.

Not that there was anything particularly wrong with Marxism as a concept, McWhinnie grinned. It just didn't work in practice. Much the same as you could say about Christianity; all right as a concept. 'I trust I don't offend you,' he tugged at his jacket-cuffs.

'Not in the slightest.'

McWhinnie looked disappointed. At either end of the mantelpiece stood marble busts of Wellington and Nelson; on the sideboard a bronze statuette of Napoleon on a rearing stallion. McWhinnie was going on about the dangers of fanaticism, totalitarianism…

'Militarism?' Danny said at last. McWhinnie beamed and wiped a bead of spittle from his lips.

'Discipline,' he said, 'made all the difference in the world.' He went on, explaining his view fully, and ended 'd'ye see?' Danny shrugged.

'Live and let live,' he mumbled, unwilling to be drawn into the old man's game.

'A most commendable sentiment,' agreed McWhinnie. 'Love thy neighbour as thyself, even better. Both admirable concepts: but not, I fear, strictly practical considerations. Not live and let live in the Burmese jungle when your neighbour is a fifth columnist with a Mauser automatic, d'ye see?' He took a sip of sherry and wiped his mouth. 'Sometimes then it's kill or be killed.'

He talked of killing in the abstract with anecdotes which were well-rehearsed and full of detail, yet something in his voice, his manner was false. Perhaps it was the rift between his acquired donnish pose and the circumstances he narrated; it was too neatly dovetailed. He was an armchair general mapping out a battlefield with sherry glasses and fine editions.

'Have you ever killed?' Danny asked, abruptly. McWhinnie faltered and stopped.

'Why do you ask?' he said.

'It seemed a natural question. I'm sorry if I offended you.'

McWhinnie smiled. '*Touché.*'

In the silence they heard the chapel bell and Danny gathered up his books, expecting to be dismissed.

'Wait.' McWhinnie began telling a story, rather a drab sort of story, about Burma during the war; only every time he got started, he stopped, as though regretting having ever started in the first place. His voice died and drifted away as he went on about the weather, the rain, all the monsoon rain in Burma. The setting sun cast deep shadows over the death mask of Gordon of Khartoum hanging on the wall behind him.

'That's very interesting,' Danny broke in as McWhinnie's voice faltered again. Time was going on, and if he didn't go soon he'd be late for Hall. But McWhinnie wouldn't let him go.

'No, no, you don't understand,' he said, 'wait until I tell you.' It was odd how insistent he became, looking up, suddenly furious, the veins in his neck standing out like drainpipes, his hands trembling like leaves.

'I took four men, my staff-sergeant, two conscripts and a native, and went up the line. It was getting dark and pissing down so that as we walked about a mile or so, our boots filled up with water. Then we saw a shape moving in the trees. I told my sergeant to call out – which he did, but there wasn't any answer. Then the native shouted something, I don't know what, but suddenly the figure stood up. I told the native to tell him to surrender, so he yelled to him again but this time the figure just backed away. The train was almost due now and we could hear it further up the track. I shouted to him again to surrender but still no answer and now we could see the train. Suddenly he dived and I, thinking there must be a detonator, shot at him. The staff sergeant shot at him and all of a sudden there was an almighty blast. By the time I came round the train had gone.

Apparently the explosion had misfired. But the strange thing was that the blighter we had shot at had completely disappeared. No sign of him anywhere.'

'So you don't know if you killed him?'

McWhinnie shook his head. 'All I know is that in the morning, when I sent my orderly to fetch the rain-butt for my shaving water, he found it full of blood. And floating on the top a turban – with a bullet-hole right through it.'

The McWhinnie review was late, but, try as he might, Danny could find little about the book to commend. The harder he looked, the more it confirmed his worst suspicions that what had once appeared innovative in McWhinnie's style had since degenerated into reflex mannerisms. The annotations were quirky, with a quirkiness that reeked not of originality but prejudice; however, to criticise the book in terms it so evidently warranted would seem not just ungrateful but foolhardy. Despite, or possibly because of his own dwindling academic powers, McWhinnie clung tenaciously to the levers of patronage. His name figured prominently among members of UGC review boards, expert panels and research award committees. McWhinnie's favourites in the field of Madoc studies were rewarded with research grants and publisher's commissions – his enemies sank without trace.

What Danny found particularly puzzling was the tiny number of new manuscripts McWhinnie had managed to unearth. What had happened to the vast hoard of unpublished material they had all been so long promised? In reality, critical opinion had long since discounted the potential value of any commentary McWhinnie had to offer; what was awaited was the secret cache of manuscripts from a private archive in Wales to which he alone had access. But in this edition the new material was negligible, consisting of three new letters, all quite brief, and a half-dozen cancelled stanzas from the *Hymn to America* which were anyway hardly different from the standard text found in the Cripps MS. Nor was it merely the absence of material that Danny was disturbed by; the more he studied these new manuscripts the more questions he found were raised. He was reluctant to name the feeling that he had about them. What was there to suspect? Yet the odd thing was how conveniently (one might almost say miraculously) they confirmed all McWhinnie's theories. There was a stanza rhapsodising on martial airs in John Gay's *Beggar's Opera*; an extended metaphor describing the disposition of French and English battle fleets, and some rejected lines from the *Hymn to America* describing the fighting at Lexington and Bunker Hill.

Danny was falling asleep in front of *Match of the Day* when the phone rang. It was Gill. It didn't occur to him until much later that she could be checking up on him.

'Gill?'

'I thought I'd see how you were.'

'Like shit's how. Where are you?'

'Sorry to hear it.'

'Yeah, you sound it.'

'There's some things I need, my drawing pens and paper.'

'Yeah yeah...' He drank the last drops from his Budweiser. 'Where are you? When are you coming back?'

'I need them for some work I'm doing.'

'You didn't answer.'

'Just tell me when you're not there.'

'What?'

'And I'll come over and get them.'

'What's wrong with now?'

'I can't make now.'

'Why? What's keeping you?'

'It's late.'

'So?' A pause. 'Where are you?'

'Just tell me when you won't be there.'

'Why?'

'I should have thought that was obvious.'

'Not to me it's not. Why? What's wrong with now?'

'This is pointless. I shouldn't have rung.'

'Just tell me what...' The phone went dead in his hand. He tried 1471 but she had withheld her number. He should have stayed in next morning, to catch her; the Department meeting was missable, but the two tutorials after it weren't. When he got back at just after five she'd been and gone. He found a message on the kitchen table suggesting a meeting at Luigi's the following night. He could pay, the note said.

There was a thunderstorm the following night and he was drenched. He got to Luigi's late, soaked through, but still there was no sign of her. A table was reserved for them – in his name, he noted. He went to the gents to dry off and came back in time to see her descending from a taxi. He hadn't seen her for almost a fortnight, and that first glimpse made his heart pound. She looked terrific in a pale dress cut low that he didn't remember; her hair swept back and glistening.

'You look fantastic,' he said. She smiled.

'You look…' she paused, consciously taking in the drenched clothes, 'like you.'

They kissed – or rather, instead of kissing him, she brushed her cheek lightly against his. It shouldn't have bothered him, but it did. Close up, he caught the expensive tang of perfume and instantly began wondering who she was wearing it for.

'Look, I'm sorry,' he said when they had ordered and were sharing a bottle of Chablis. He would have preferred red, but anything to please her. She didn't reply.

'What do I have to do?'

She asked about the Madoc conference. Was he going?

'Why?'

'I just wondered,' she gave him the faintest smile. Suddenly everything fitted into place.

'You've talked to Carstairs, haven't you?'

'I did pop in one morning,' she replied, asking him to pass the rolls.

'And he told you about the Madoc thing.'

'He may have mentioned it, yes.'

'Bloody Madoc.'

'You're not going?'

'What do you care?'

'Just making conversation.'

Over dessert he apologised again and tried, unsuccessfully, to find out where she was living. What could he do to convince her? Couldn't she see how upset she'd made him?

'I'm very sorry,' she said, sounding anything but.

'Is it over? Have you left me? Tell me...' He put out his hand for hers; she left it for a moment, then pulled back to finish her profiteroles. No, it wasn't over, she said. And no, she wasn't seeing anybody else.

'I didn't ask,' he said.

'Not with words,' she answered. She just wanted time, she said, and drank her coffee. Just time.

3

A Welsh Companion

'...*On the far side of the B4521, a minor road leads up a sharp incline to Nightingale Hurst, which can also be reached via Plynlimon and the B4347. This fine historic mansion now houses the administrative offices of the European Center of the Order of Primitive Brethren, but can be visited, under official supervision, on bank holidays and at weekends from June until September. Nightingale Hurst was acquired by the Pendower family during the reign of Henry VII when Owen Pendower, long time supporter of the Tudor cause, was appointed Recorder and Grand Constable of the Marches. Following the death of Pendower's only son, Giles, in a hunting accident on Plynlimon Fawr, the estate was purchased by Thomas ap Simon of Gwent, whose family maintained the Hurst as a bastion of the Royalist cause throughout the Civil Wars. The history and reputation of the Hurst are now most famously associated with the poet Thomas Madoc and his circle, the so-called 'Nightingale Group' who lived and wrote here during the period 1793–6. It was in the Temple of Virtue, on the far side of the lake, that the poet Madoc tragically died on Midsummer's Eve 1796.*

Nightingale Hurst is neither sublime nor picturesque; yet, as one approaches closely, one recognises that few Welsh mansions more accurately represent the vicissitudes of architectural fashion over five centuries. Visitors familiar with the Hurst only from Abigail Pengelly's atmospheric descriptions in The Last Nightingale *(1862) may be surprised by a number of discrepancies owing to Miss Pengelly's licence. The park and gardens are very fine, containing the sole survivors of the first larches to be grown in Wales, presented to George Madoc as seedlings by the Duke of Argyll in 1748; also an artificial lake and elegant bridge built by John Standish (1760) and some curious eighteenth-century griffins' heads brought from London. Capability Brown was responsible for the landscaping, though, for some reason, the National Trust handbook omits his name – almost a relief when one thinks of the number of Capability Brown parks up and down the country. Just to the north of the Nightingale estate, the B4347 leads along the Pennyburn valley where, in Celtic times, a timber bridge carried the Devil's Causeway over the stream...'*

Manoeuvring her case before her body, Professor Terry Franks backed into the plate-glass doors of Parry Madoc Hall and found herself in a foyer that was dark and smelt of stale tobacco. Professor Franks came from Oregon, and her ideas of fun did not include conferences on Thomas Madoc – least of all in Wales. But in a less than friendly exchange of letters, her university administration had informed her that if her bursary were not quickly followed by a publisher's contract, she would soon be without a job. Her sabbatical year in Oxford had been taken up by an impetuous affair; hence, with barely two months of her year in Britain left, she found herself backing into this bleak university residence in a desperate search for something to form the basis of a book.

Terry was twenty-eight and had promised herself she would make it East by thirty.

The porters' desk was empty, littered with scraps of paper torn into tiny strips, scrawled with indecipherable markings. Calling cards from taxi firms and Chinese takeaways stuck in the rim of the glass partition to the switchboard; an irregular pattern of keys hung on a green board at the back; a grubby firemanual, a gummy biro, a copy of *Sporting Life* lay on the ledge. At the present rate of progress, she'd be lucky if she made East river. She faked a cough but no one came. She was about to leave when there was a voice.

'*Mad dog?*'

The sound, more like a parrot-squawk than human speech, seemed to come from nowhere. She turned and saw a wide expanse of grey trousers, followed by an off-white shirt, yellow teeth and wide red ears emerging, bent over, from a cupboard.

'*Mad dog?*'

The porter stood up, uncurled his lips in an unconvincing show of welcome to disclose teeth the colour of bamboo. Professor Franks nodded.

'Sure,' she said, 'Madoc.' She waved her registration papers and leant across to sign the form – noticing, with distaste, little bubbles of saliva on the grey surface of his tongue. She asked where to find the room assigned to her in Block B.

'Block B?' he snatched the key back, examined it against his list, examined her, then returned it, grinning rather ominously.

'Well?'

The porter unfolded himself like a Mexican wave and pointed to a tower-block about half a mile away.

It was warm and, resting at a seat halfway up Pendower Rise, Terry took out a pack of cigarettes and read through the conference notes. Once there had been shepherds' cottages all across these fields, but George Madoc flattened them in pursuit of his improvements. He dammed up the stream to form an ornamental lake, fashioned a cascade on which stone fauns and naiads frolicked, and erected a Temple of Virtue which, apart from the doric columns and a sculpted freize depicting the labours of Aesculapius, was modelled on the *Maison Carré*. He crowned the perspective by placing an heptagonal mausoleum at the end of an avenue of cypresses, each face surmounted by a tympanum celebrating one of the seven torments of surgery. As he gazed from his library windows he declared that he enjoyed a view 'as remedially composed as a landscape by Poussin'. A notorious hypochondriac, Madoc spent his life in extended litigation with doctors and, remarkably for a man who constantly declared he felt the chill hand of Death upon him, survived till eighty-four. Even then he was, to all appearances, in the rudest health when he was mown down by a runaway post-chaise on the descent from the Brecon Beacons. Professor Franks squeezed out her cigarette, gazed around the grassy hills and, for a moment, felt something akin to tranquillity. But only for an instant – then it was back to her folder in the pursuit of a possible research topic. George Madoc's only literary achievement, the mock-epic *Aesculapiad*, a Popean satire on doctors, was full of pseudo-classical parodies, and the Hurst was decorated throughout with similar acrostics. Embrasures and balustrades were ornamented with a profusion of mouldings in the forms of pills and plasters, blisters and clysters. Busts of Galen and Hippocrates cropped up in the most unexpected places, their names anagrammatised on lintels and chimney-braces, their faces glowering down like gargoyles above the leaden water pipes. The caduceus of Apollo twined around the central staircase and a heraldic frieze of forceps rampant surrounded the oriel windows and rose above the mantelpiece. Professor Franks wondered when the last George Madoc book was published and very much regretted her detestation of the heroic couplet.

She got up, resumed her climb and noticed, as she did so, the breeze-blocks which made up the Residence walls were fissured and would soon melt over these limestone hills like architectural fondue. The conference was a last-minute decision; it had been this or Walter Scott. Lugging her case behind her as she climbed the stairs she wondered if she had made the right decision. She heaved her case onto the final landing but it struck a banister, teetered for an instant, then toppled forward.

'Shit!'

She lunged forward, squashing the case against the stairs with too much pressure; a hinge burst, a tangle of black stockings spiralled down the stairwell, followed by a bottle of Chanel that dropped straight down several flights and landed with a loud bang on the floor.

'Having trouble?' A man appeared, who knelt down, and together they dragged the case back without losing anything else. Terry brushed herself down, shoved her underwear back inside the case and thanked him. 'Don't worry about the stuff down there, I'll get it for you.' he kindly offered. The guy's name was Danny and he roomed across the corridor from her, which was apparently contrary to every regulation. The Primitive Brethren were very hot on segregation; Block B was strictly 'Men only'. They worked out it was her name which caused all the confusion. The primitive ladies were sure to get into a flap about it.

'I'll tell them not to worry,' she said, as he helped her get the case into her room, 'I don't mind the odd cock-up.'

They agreed to meet up in an hour, which gave her time to wash (in cold water; the Primitive Brethren seemed to think hot water a diabolical device) and finish reading up her notes about the place. After George Madoc died, the Hurst passed to grandson Thomas who, together with his sister Jane, romanticised the Temple of Virtue and removed its columns, redesigning it as a charming Gothic dairy where they could read aloud their rustic ballads, dress in peasant costume and milk a few tame cows. They held boating parties there, sitting up late and reading by firelight. It was on the jetty that Thomas Madoc's body was discovered on midsummer night, 1796. In the nineteenth century the Hurst briefly housed an inglorious public school, when the former Temple of Virtue served as communal bathhouse-cum-pavilion. It was, reputedly, the scene of many nocturnal entertainments among the boys, inspired by its Romantic association (of which the school's proprietors, both clergymen, denied all knowledge). When, as a result of some such escapade, the son of an India Office Under-Secretary was found dead with his brains dashed out, enquiries led to the rapid closure of the school. Interest was revived with the publication (in 1862) of Abigail Pengelly's novel *The Last Nightingale*, which was such a success she was able to purchase the estate; but, rather than exert herself by resisting decay, she seemed positively to welcome it. On her death, it descended to a distant cousin in South Africa, who saw no reason to relinquish the veldt for a draughty Welsh prison (as the place was accurately described to him). For several decades the fabric decayed until, eventually, in the 1950s, it was purchased by the Order of Primitive Brethren to serve as their European base. The Temple of Virtue was demolished in order to make way for the Parry Madoc Halls of Residence, leaving only the legend which once adorned the Temple's lintel preserved as a stone memorial: *sic transit glo–*.

At four o'clock Professor Franks knocked on Danny's door. She was rewarded with a bundle of tights and the information that her scent bottle had smashed.

'Thought so,' she said. The whole building was haunted by an odour of Chanel No 5.

'You can always use mine,' he said, holding up a bottle of *Pour Monsieur*.

'I'll bear it in mind.'

In the intervening hour she had read all about him in the conference folder. She said she admired his work as she handed him his shirts out of his suitcase (washed and ironed by Sketchley's, she noted) and resumed her cross-legged posture on his bed. Danny didn't know whether the remark was genuine. In London he had never come across anybody who had read his book on Madoc, or realised that it was on George, not Thomas. Not many people even knew there *was* a George; but then, this was a Madoc conference.

'Is this edition the McWhinnie?' she asked, stretching across his socks and pants for a slim blue hardback.

'Oh yes, it's...'

'May I?' she said, picking it up and noticing how her fingernails matched his jockey-shorts exactly. 'It's so thin! I thought this was supposed to be the big one?' Their eyes met again. There was a pause in which both thought of *risqué* rejoinders, but said nothing.

'What happened to all the manuscripts? I thought this was supposed to be based on them?'

'Good question. Maybe you'd better ask him.'

Terry laughed and threw the book back in his case. 'Do you have any booze up here? I could really do with a beer.' Danny shook his head.

'Pity,' she said. 'From what I hear, that could be a big mistake.' She grinned and leant forward, letting him catch a glimpse of black bra-strap beneath her black silk blouse.

As Hugo Carstairs opened up the boot of his Volvo Estate there was a snapping sound and the lock dropped off. He was parked in a muddy lay-by on the south side of the A465, just north, if he judged it right, of the College grounds. He stared as the stupid thing rolled and settled among old oil and petrol cans and cursed. Was *this* what they meant by reliability? It wasn't just the boot-lock which irked him. Somehow the map readings were all wrong, though he couldn't for the life of him see why. He spread out the ordnance survey map across the Volvo bonnet, anchoring the corners down with old copies of the

Michelin guide. It was conceivable he'd got the wrong lay-by. The nuisance was created by some damned fool, the Forestry Commission or some well-heeled tax-dodger, covering Llanwhynn Hill with a plantation of totally incongruous pines. Apart from the fact that they were completely out of sympathy with the local ecology, they utterly ruined the view over the bare heath. How people got away with it he couldn't understand. A battered Morris Minor drew up beside him in the lay-by with a Plaid Cymru sticker across the top of its windscreen. A middle-aged woman in sensible tweeds, her grey hair tied back in a bun, got out and strode towards him.

'You there,' she shouted in the booming tones of an English public school matron, 'just what do you think you're doing?'

Carstairs was taken aback by her directness. 'I'm sorry,' he said.

'I should jolly well think you are. After the petition and everything. You people!' She placed her hand down flat on the map. 'Well, that's more than enough of that!'

Carstairs watched, incredulous, as she yanked the map away, scattering the Michelin guides to Italy and France into the mud. 'Look here,' he said, 'what is all this?'

'Don't try to fool me,' she warned, and wagged her finger.

'I haven't the faintest idea what you're talking about. Give me that back.'

'No fear.'

'Give me it back.'

'Not likely.'

Carstairs assumed his haughtiest pedagogic manner. 'Madam,' he said, 'I don't know who you are or what particular delusion you may be labouring under, but that map happens to be mine.' So saying, he hurled himself and made a sudden snatch for it. But she easily evaded his clumsy lunge and he only succeeded in winding himself on a wing mirror. 'This is daylight robbery,' he groaned, rubbing his aching ribs.

'Exactly,' she crowed, 'and what have you people have been doing in this country for more years than I care to remember? Stealing it from under our very noses.'

'Madam,' he said, attempting to stand upright, though the pain was very severe, 'I am Professor Carstairs from London University.'

'And I am Councillor Penelope Powell-Davies. When we said direct action, we meant it. We're having no more of your bulldozers.'

With as much vehemence as he could muster in his pained condition, Carstairs contemptuously denied any association whatsoever with bulldozers. His field, he assured her, was Romantic poetry. He had published books on Coleridge and Madoc. She was not impressed.

'With a theodolite?' she asked, with a disbelieving sneer. Now even Carstairs could see the funny side;

the theodolite in question had been left with him by an architect who was supposed to be landscaping his drive. It was not, he readily conceded, the customary critical tool, but then he was not the customary critic. He explained, briefly, about the conference. As a matter of fact, he concluded, he couldn't agree with her more about bulldozers and juggernauts. If she cared to consult his book on Madoc (of which the local library had a signed copy), she would find a section deploring the sheer ugliness of the M47 motorway which cut right across an ancient and sacred Celtic track.

Still Powell-Davies was on her guard. She could tell a charmer when she met one. He wasn't getting round her that easily. She clung tenaciously to the map. She would speak to Mrs Llampreys at the library and if – she stressed the word – *if* she confirmed what he said, then possibly he could have it back tomorrow. 'If not...'

She climbed back inside her car and slammed the door. There was a loud crunch of gears as she lurched away leaving a thick trail of blue exhaust fumes behind her.

Terry and Danny stood outside the Pendower Lounge reading a notice that informed them it would open at 6 p.m. It was a little before five and they were both very dry. There was a machine which dispensed a liquid beverage. Danny, not having heard of *Pola Cola*, was rather wary.

'Why not?' said Terry, borrowing coins from him (she'd left her bag in her room), and got herself a cup. They sat in the vast window at one end of the lounge looking out while she did her best to drink it.

'What's it like?'

'Nice. Quite nice. Have some.'

He had some, more to share her cup than for the liquid. He turned up his nose.

'You don't like it?'

'Don't mind me. I don't like coke.'

Hancock and Carstairs were on the list of those attending. For him, he said with a faint touch of irony, it would be home from home.

'That's nice,' she said, finishing her *Pola Cola*.

'Do you think so?' he said, looking at her, meaningfully. He always thought the best thing about conferences was meeting new people. She refused the obvious bait and said she 'didn't know', having not attended many. She shook out her dark hair behind her. They talked about the McWhinnie edition of Madoc he'd reviewed (Thomas Madoc, not George – she quickly gathered – who wrote blank verse, which was much more suitable for her purpose). It should be in the Sunday paper.

'We must be sure and get it,' she said, and asked him what he thought of it.

'Not much. Though, of course, I haven't said so. He's what you might call an old –' he paused, trying to think of the right word.

'Friend?' she volunteered.

'Not friend, exactly – nor colleague either. He taught me.'

'Ah, I see,' said Terry, rather too quickly. It was difficult, or rather Danny *felt* it difficult to articulate the precise degree of intimacy he felt for McWhinnie – and, in her easy formulas, he felt he was being mocked.

'I doubt it,' he said, quite sharply, and Terry knew she had stepped into something.

'I'm sorry,' she said. 'I only meant you want to protect him. I understand. College honour and so forth...'

Danny wouldn't be pacified, for Terry had struck pretty close to the truth. 'No,' he said, and stood up. 'I didn't think you would...'

'Explain it to me,' she said, but Danny shook his head.

'Morris will be lecturing,' he said.

'You said you didn't want to go,' she said, still sitting where she was.

'I must've changed my mind,' said Danny, making for the door.

'Nightingale Hurst, perched on the brow of an abbreviated limestone cliff in the wettest corner of Wales. The prevailing weather was from the north-west, swirling across the Irish sea before howling over Plynlimon Fawr; but a trough in the valley bordering the Hurst and encompassing its woodlands seemed to suck down all its moisture and hold it, like a fen.

Even when there was no rain, which was rare enough, the air was filled with damp, a fine grey clammy mist permeating everything. On the flint gate-posts guarding the driveway to the Hurst stood a pair of fearsome heraldic beasts, bearing shields and armorial crests; their precise species – whether phoenixes, griffins or wyverns – was now indecipherable; their talons and beaks were worn away by the perpetual wet. A slime-green lichen spread across their breasts and fringed their stony scales; their wings were cracked and stained. The walls around the Hurst harboured a profusion of parasitic growths coloured all shades of dung, from jet-black to a lurid green, while on their sheltered inner-sides exotic spidery growths of yellow lichens, rash gaudy reds and purple hare-bells...'

Danny watched the lecturer, Grant Morris, lean across the lectern, tuck his shirt-cuffs inside his jacket and tip his glasses a half-inch further down his nose. 'Remember,' he said, dropping his voice, squinting above his audience's heads, obviously enjoying himself immensely, 'that was written in 1862, almost seventy years after the last major modification to the Hurst.'

He paused and gazed towards the Gothic windows at the rear of the room, where a plaster bust of Llewellyn the Last and a portrait of Sir Gareth ap Williams stared back at him.

'You can still see the very walls she describes in such minute botanical detail,' he pointed, marking out the perimeter of the campus; 'the stretch along the Aberdovey Road is particularly well preserved. But observe the careful colour-coding of the parasites. This is not naturalism, you see – far from it. This is not some pre-Darwinian expression of botanical evolution, but rather a subtle pattern of cultural allusions, a kind of aesthetic code whose full significance is only to be deciphered by those with a thorough comprehension of Celtic mythology. What we have, in fact, is a kind of allegory which parades the forbidden symbols of an oppressed culture under the very noses of the English. Vicars' wives who contributed in their hundreds to elegant subscription editions; governesses who borrowed it from circulating libraries and school-teachers who bought the twopenny reprint, all fondly believed that they were enjoying a charming fable, a fantasy romance. Little did they realise what they were reading was in fact subversive propaganda! –'

He had a way of leaning forward and pausing, in the middle of a sentence, before sweeping on to its conclusion, which conveyed an immense sense of self-satisfaction. Lecturing was in Morris' blood: his grandfather had preached from Presbyterian pulpits in Balsall Heath; his father had declaimed from the back of NUM vans trundling the Heads of the Valleys road from Neath to Pontypridd. Little beads of sweat stood out like pearls as he flourished the subversive novel over all their heads. Yet, despite the urgency of his delivery, his audience were drowsy, not expecting anything demanding on their first afternoon. As it was, barely half of them had arrived. Trains via Cardiff and Brecon were delayed, and even with the thoughtful provision of coaches to ferry delegates the thirteen miles from the station, the bulk of those attending weren't expected till after five. Acoustics in the Hurst, with its high ceilings and panelled walls, were not good, and a faint murmur of Morris' voice carried from the Llewellyn library to the entrance hall, where two Primitive Brethren (female) from the welcoming committee had pitched their trestle-table between bronze statues of the founding Brothers and handed out name-tags, keys, folders and a paperback edition of the New Testament. Groups gathered around the registration table caught only the upbeat of each sentence; the antithetical cadence as his voice dropped away was lost to them. The result, a series of short gasps, was like the sound of a man drowning.

Danny sat on a plastic chair at the rear of the library, listening to Morris speaking a bit too fast for his audience as if teasing them towards some final revelation. He was altogether too sure of himself. There was something contrived about his way of stage-managing his arguments, as though he were a conjuror rather than an academic.

'In the spring of 1797,' said Morris, 'a squadron of four French ships landed at Y Cwm – Fishguard – full of soldiers from the *Deuxieme Legion*. These were the vanguard of a French invasion fleet. As we know, that invasion never happened and the French troops

56

soon surrendered. However, during the time they occupied this small corner of western Wales there is evidence to suggest that they were visited, and may even have been assisted by Madoc and his sister Jane. This was when Madoc composed the *Basque Cantoes*, which are full of revolutionary nationalist sentiments. It seems clear the French invasion of 1797 was the final factor leading to the break-up of the Nightingale Group that summer. We know there were English government spies based at Haverfordwest and Milford Haven with orders to keep an eye on Madoc, and some of their reports make fascinating reading. There is good reason to suppose that Madoc was the mysterious "man in black" who crops up in accounts of the Spithead mutiny in April. According to one spy this "man in black" addressed a meeting in a Portsmouth pub, denounced the war and private property, and urged them to throw off "the chains of despotic rule". Another time this "man in black" seems to have had rather too much to drink – which would square with Madoc. He is reported to have declaimed a seditious poem; but unfortunately the spy assigned to follow him had rather a blind spot where poetry was concerned. He made valiant efforts to memorise as much of the poem as he could, but it's clear that anything metaphorical passed him by. All he managed to scribble in his notebook is a garbled series of melodramatic flourishes including *secret sources, smooth-faced tyrants, guilty Pharoahs* (the spelling of which is a wonder to behold) and *bloody pimp* which might equally be "bloody pomp". From all of which farrago I think we can just make out (though it's hardly a compliment to Madoc to say so) the dim outlines of some central stanzas of the *Basque Cantoes*. As we know from entries in Jane's diary, he finally completed a first draft of the *Cantoes* that June, just before his tragic death, here, in the lake.'

Morris finished his lecture, shuffled the pages and ran a hand through his thinning hair. There was a general spatter of applause and some people at the back got up and left the room. A girl in round glasses stood up, an alpaca sweater and long brown hair shadowing her face like a cowl.

'I was wondering,' she said softly, blushing slightly.

'Yes?' Morris' fingers fumbled with the knot of his tie and he tried to look her in the eyes, but sun glinted off her spectacles and veiled them in light.

'You never mentioned the druids,' she looped back a length of hair behind her ears and looked about the room for supporters. Her eyes, large and dark, bulged like fish-optics behind her pebble glasses. 'Surely they are the key to the *Basque Cantoes*. The odes are Celtic mythology, the old religion. Madoc himself was a druid, he must have been…'

A patronising grin spread across Morris' face. 'Been reading Samuelson, have you?' he said. 'Well, it's an interesting *theory*, I suppose – but where's the evidence?'

'He was killed on midsummer's day,' the girl in glasses quickly retorted.

'He *died* on midsummer's day,' said Morris, pushing all his papers into a manilla envelope and moving towards the door.

'But...' the girl's hair flopped forward, as she lowered her gaze and was about to speak again, but Morris cut her off.

'Must go,' he said, 'sorry. Maybe we can discuss it later.' He held out a hand to guide her from the room; but she stood stock-still, gazing at the pattern of shadows, like a circle of rose leaves, that the sun cast from the extractor fan onto the parquet floor.

'If you're looking for the real shampoo, old son, forget it. Welcome to Camp Colditz!'

The figure in grey flannels lurching out to greet him from between a pair of Hippocratic effigies was Hancock – face purple, speech blurred, tie dangling loosely from his open collar like a noose. He tugged Danny by the sleeve.

'Not going to introduce me?'

Reluctantly Danny introduced Hancock to Terry, whom he'd met coming out of Morris' lecture. She was less hostile now than she had been – or he thought she had been – in the Pendower Lounge, and he was keen to put that episode behind him. Hancock came forward to take her hand, but rocked against the trestle table and clutched Danny's arm to steady himself.

'Strictly TT the lot of 'em.' He whispered so close his breath tickled Danny's ear. He straightened up, winked and tapped the side of his nose, confidentially.

'I hear they got a special dispensation from the Witch-Doctor in Chief, on the hotline to –' he pointed heavenwards. 'And the message came –' he lifted his voice and yelled: '"Let there be booze!"' Several delegates turned to look at him. 'Oh yes!' he went on, 'they really pushed the boat out and got *two* bottles of the widow. Two!' he raised his eyebrows. 'Luckily I took certain precautions,' and he opened up his jacket to reveal a half-bottle of Glenfiddich tucked inside. 'Fancy a nip?' he said, and turned to Terry.

'Sure,' she took the bottle, had a swig and passed it on to Danny, whose sharp intake of breath proved it wasn't what he was used to.

'For future reference,' she said, handing the bottle back to Hancock, 'I prefer bourbon.' His face glowed. 'My dear,' he said, 'you are here for an education.'

He bowed and turned to go. 'But the reception?' she said. He gave a careful thumbs-down sign.

Not quite his *tasse de thé*, he said, slurring his words and almost colliding with a rhododendron bush. 'Don't be fooled by the gold foil and popping corks,' he yelled. 'Stuff tastes like lucozade.'

In which he was correct. The stuff tasted *just* like lucozade. Two beaming rows of the Brethren dispensed two gleaming rows of gold-topped bottles with a symmetry that was alarming. Meanwhile they repeated the *immense* delight they took in hosting such a *prestigious* literary event. They had a way of italicising every adjective as though reading from an illuminated script. Christian names were obligatory.

Christopher hoped that Danny's stay at the Hurst would be tranquil and *fulfilling*, while Vijay assured Terry that if there was anything she was requiring, the Brethren would be *joyful* to perform it. The room where the reception took place was decorated in accordance with the Primitive Brethren's taste and resembled a pre-war Odeon cinema. It was hung and carpeted entirely in plush purple, while the ceiling was cerulean blue with a sprinkling of gold dust thrown carelessly across it. From its centre hung and slowly revolved a huge golden cross.

'Like a 1930s dance-hall,' said Danny.

'Or a bordello,' Terry replied.

The room filled with baggy suits, cotton blouses and lots of plastic conference badges, most of whom knew Danny. Terry was required to meet a pink hollyhock frock called Juliet and a polka-dot bow-tie called George. An expensive pair of eye-shades stared at her – which belonged to Grant Morris who, having changed clothes since lecturing, now dressed from Hollywood *circa* 1950 and lounged as though posed by a grand piano. As they approached, he stood, pumped Danny's hand and fixed his eyes on Terry.

'Before you say a word,' he said, 'I want you to know it's not my fault. I am going to get a sign made and hang it round my neck – IT'S NOT MY FAULT. Actually, if you drink enough of the stuff, it has a kind of numbing effect. You must be?...' He held out his hand.

'Do you actually play that thing?' she said, ignoring his advance and pointing at the piano.

'Well no, actually.'

'Pity. Weren't you rather hard on the druid woman?'

Morris removed his shades. 'You surely aren't one of these New Age types?'

'I hope I'm not a *type* at all,' she said.

Turning, she led Danny up a narrow staircase towards a minstrels' gallery, where she sat, took off her shoes and began massaging her toes. How many of these people did he actually know? she said. She hated formal shoes, but guessed this was the sort of occasion you were supposed to wear them. She couldn't decide whether she could be bothered to get to know any of them. 'Who's that guy?' she said. 'The one giving off all the steam. McWhinnie?'

'Samuelson,' said Dan.

Somehow Samuelson appeared to be not one man simply, but a crowd which, at a glance, you knew you did not wish to be part of. He seemed to have not arms, but tentacles, curling and uncurling restlessly about him. His body was not entirely contained within his clothes, but had ankles and wrists projecting several inches and a paunch swelling ominously above his waistband. Samuelson was a conversational prize-fighter, an omnivore of gossip, scandal and innuendo; you could see it in his posture as he stood, beard seamed with sweat, taking on not one, not two but three simultaneous verbal bouts, violently throwing his whole body into each. Suddenly their host, the Dean of the Order of Primitive Brethren, stood on the dais, raised his arms for quiet, and delivered them a few unctuous mid-Western terms of greeting. Jesus, he declared, would be watchin' over their deliberations and would be with them in all they said and did. The Dean probably didn't mean to worry them with his hair as neat and golden as a new-mown prairie, and his blazer of a dazzling blue to match his eyes. But somehow he did.

'You're younger than I imagined,' Terry whispered in a way Danny wasn't sure was complimentary. That was exactly how she meant it, she said. 'You get a sort of mental image when you read somebody's book – you know, a sort of picture.'

'Bald, decrepit, toothless…'

'Not exactly,' she smiled. 'More like Philip Larkin. Most English guys I read sound like Philip Larkin – that whining blend of self-righteousness and pity.' She stopped.

'You don't mind me saying this?'

'Mind?' said Danny in mock innocence. What was there to mind? He was only sorry to disappoint her.

'That's it!' she yelled and clapped her hands so people down below looked up at her. She lowered her voice. That was it exactly – sort of pompous and terribly English.

Then it was the chaplain's turn to address them. The chaplain was completely black – black face, black hands, black gown. In his hands was a large black bible, and his voice, entirely Welsh, was thick with memories of coal dust. He was the only black in the room. He threw his bible open with a flourish, closed his eyes and stared for a while at the ceiling, waiting for a total silence before he began to speak. They were here, he understood, to study *Mad*-oc (placing a heavy emphasis on the first syllable). *Mad*-oc's dreams of the utopia. He opened his eyes and focused on the nearest group of people, including Samuelson and a lady in a Laura Ashley frock. Well, the utopia was not a word he found in his bible. As he understood it – and he could be wrong, not being an expert on the subject (he paused) like *them* – but as he understood it, this utopia was a kind of heaven upon earth. He paused and looked at them. There was not a sound to be heard. An earthly paradise. So why was it not mentioned in his bible? Those other words were. Words like heaven, paradise, Eden, Jerusalem, the promised land. But not utopia. Every supposed utopia he'd ever heard of – and he wasn't an expert: they were the experts, not him – used all those other terms fairly freely. It was Eden, it was paradise, it was a land of milk and honey. But what would that mean – an earthly paradise? What would it be like? Well, if they cared to look in this book – not by *Mad*-oc but by God – and he flung his bible open – and they happened to look at Genesis, they would see that there *had* actually once been such an earthly paradise. The Garden of

Eden. '*And the Lord God planted a Garden eastward in Eden: and there he put the man whom he had formed. And out of the ground made the Lord God to grow every tree that is pleasant to the sight and good for food.*' But what happened to that earthly paradise? What was the story of the Garden of Eden and of our first parents' banishment from this early state of primal bliss? He was sure he didn't need to remind them that the devil – in a serpent's form – tempted Eve, who ate of the Tree of Knowledge. And she gave Adam also to eat of it, so that they were banished from the only paradise that Man has ever known. Hence the Fall. Hence Chaos. Hence misery, contagion, poverty – hence wars and suffering and exploitation. For a full five minutes he rattled through a catalogue of miseries before slamming the bible shut and striding from the dais. There was a sudden, total silence.

'It's not my fault,' said Morris, 'if people insist on making heaven unattractive. I mean, if God hadn't meant us to think, why did he give us brains?'

'*She*,' said Terry, which so surprised him that he took off his shades.

'Oh God,' said Morris, 'you're not one of *those*?'

'No,' she said. 'Personally I don't believe in her – only I'm pretty sure it's a *her* I don't believe in.'

One of the younger brethren came and whispered something in Morris' ear.

'OK, OK, I'm coming,' he frowned. 'Just remember that *it's not my fault.*'

After he'd gone Terry turned to Danny. 'Look, about these manuscripts,' she said, 'McWhinnie's stash. I've been thinking. His private archive in Wales has to be here, right?' Danny hesitated.

'Assuming it ever existed,' he said.

'You think he made it up?'

'Who knows? I wouldn't put it past him.'

'Your friend Carstairs seems to think they're here.'

'What?'

'I was talking to him earlier, or rather, he was talking to me. He said if they're anywhere they must be here.'

'I see.'

'You disagree?'

'Then why didn't he publish them?'

'*That's* what I want to find out.'

Danny wished her the best of luck. Terry pulled a face.

'Come on, it's worth a shot. I'm game if you are.'

'For what, exactly?'

'To look for them. I'll make a bet with you that they're here. Twenty pounds, fifty pounds, what you will.'

Danny smiled. For some reason money had never been particularly compelling, he said.

'Oh, so what?...' They looked at each other, grinning.

'OK,' she said, 'you help me look for them...'

'And?'

'And remember, if we do find anything, we share copyright on what we find.'

'I meant, what's my incentive?'

She made a face. 'I'm sure we'll think of something.'

Outside they met Hancock loitering behind a rhododendron. 'Just thought I'd let you know, I've appointed myself Captain of the Escape Committee. I've been doing a preliminary recce. Nearest watering-hole's a dismal sort of dive. I've located somewhere pretty decent in a place called –' he dug inside his pocket for a map and flapped it out before them. 'Are you lot any good with these Welsh names? All Lls and Wws? It's a bit of a hike, I grant you, but should be worth a shuftie. I was thinking of making a little expedition tomorrow. The goons lock up at ten o'clock pip emma, but I suppose we could always shin over the wall.'

4

The invitation to Jane Simmons' private view came as something of a shock, but Gill was prepared to overlook Jane's tendency to crow which, even at the age of twelve, set her apart from less distinguished classmates. She instantly accepted, saying in a hastily scribbled postscript that she 'hoped Jane wouldn't mind' if she brought somebody new. She smiled as she licked the envelope, trying to imagine Jane's expression. The invitation had been addressed to her but, in a flourish of red ink across one corner, Jane had scribbled 'Gill & friend', evidently hoping that Danny might be persuaded to attend. She would be sadly disappointed.

Instead, Gill brought Alice, whose sudden flight to Greece had been immediately cancelled when Gill phoned up and asked to stay. Dying to discover the reason, Alice set her endlessly demanding friend on Rhodes aside and put herself entirely at Gill's command. Nothing worse – she breathed to Gill on their first evening – than having to admit to loads of ghastly explanations. They sat together in the tiny kitchen of her flat, eating a delicate linguine *al burro* and drinking Italian red. Particularly – she paused, hooking her features into an implausible grin – of an intimate nature. When she left Steve, she couldn't bear to look at *those parts* of herself for at least a month. Luckily she had the kind of pubic hair that grew back quite quickly. Would Gill like espresso, or would she settle for instant? Gill didn't respond to Alice's promptings, but did mention Baxter's painting, which was clearly a *version* of the Norwich school. She herself rather doubted if it was a Crome or Cotman – but that was absolutely no reason for Danny to use it to goad Carstairs.

'So?' said Alice, to whom this sounded like displaced memory.

'I moved out,' said Gill, adding that instant would be fine.

She was horrified when she found out Alice had cancelled her holiday. That was ridiculous, two weeks in Greece! Of course she must go, she said, or she would feel horribly guilty. She argued against the cancellation so vehemently Alice asked if she would like to go instead. It wouldn't bother Marguerite – who'd hardly notice, being drunk most of the time. Gill mentioned the invitation from Jane Simmons as a reason to decline, but already she sensed that staying here with Alice wasn't going to work. She needed perfect calm. The idea of a fortnight doing nothing but water fuchsias and clematis had been her idea of bliss. She tried intimating this to Alice, who instantly agreed; but her idea of calm, and Alice's, were two quite separate things. On the third morning of her stay, Gill bought the *Evening Standard* and started looking through it for flat-share adverts.

Jane Simmons didn't have a style of her own, but had married a rich lawyer, twice her age, who financed her exhibitions which he wrote off as company losses. For five years Jane would favour a particular vogue; the present exhibition was of paintings of her most recent vogue specialising, like Hockney, in slim young men in dark glasses against azure swimming pools.

'Gill!'

'Jane!'

They kissed like the blades of scissors meeting.

'You remember Alice?'

'Of *course*,' said Jane, who hadn't the least idea who 'Alice' was. She even allowed herself to wonder, advancing her elegantly manicured head to peck at Alice's oily cheek, if she were one of Gillian's jokes. Her skin looked vaguely as though it might be detachable.

'I was at Woburn,' said Alice, 'before they closed it.'

'Of course,' murmured Jane, who wandered off to greet a woman who was older, wealthier and more interested in art. Gill and Alice stood before a large picture of a solitary man in handsome shades and tight black shorts before a dazzlingly blue swimming pool. He was a very manly man. It seemed vaguely indecent of them to be looking so intently at him.

'Reminds me of –' Alice began.

'Just what I was thinking,' said Gill, and they both burst out laughing.

The last lecture of the day was given by Max Gibbon, dressed in black leather trousers, black leather tie and brash check shirt. Formerly Gibbon had been on excellent terms with Morris, the two cultivating reputations as Marxist *enfants terribles* at Cambridge and collaborating on a notorious book of essays. There was the most terrific rumpus when Gibbon's Assistant Lectureship hadn't been renewed and he was forced to get a post at Birmingham. Gibbon's style of delivery was quick and nervous, spoken in a flat Northern monotone and mixing metaphors as if to prove his contempt for literary decorum. He made short, jerky movements of his arms, smashing his right fist into his left palm as he grappled with the veil of mystification that surrounded the so-called Nightingale Group – a veil systematically woven by Establishment critics who wished to conceal the true revolutionary significance of their works. For nearly two centuries they had been at it, bowdlerising and castrating their writings in order to embalm them in a safe, dead haven: Art.

'Look,' he said, holding up the slim navy volume, '*Madoc* – I had to read *this* at school. The editor, Professor P.R.Q. James, made Madoc safe by simply omitting anything subversive. You won't find the *Basque Cantoes* here; nor the *Hymn to America* or *Anarchy in Arcadia*. You won't find any *ideas* at all. Or this –' he held up the Penguin selection of Madoc and Williams edited by Gwendolen Glover, 'listen to what Miss Glover says: "*Sadly one is forced to confess that when straying from lyric verse into the realms of political satire, Madoc's poetry betrays an immaturity which must bring a blush to the cheeks of even his most ardent admirers.*" Or here –' and he displayed the new edition of Madoc, 'the editor of this declares that the *Basque Cantoes* and the *Hymn to America* are "lamentable evidence that rare poetic genius can coexist with utter political naivety"'. Gibbon slammed the book shut. Time and again it was the same. Desperate attempts to keep them safely within their own special reservation of Art with a capital A – the same harping on exotic or pastoral motifs – pantheism, mysticism, druidism – the same desire to present them as somehow not quite grown up. Geniuses perhaps, but naive and innocent, like children. But nothing could be further from the truth. Everything about them – their writings, their principles, their love of nature and their campaigns – were intensely political. What was truly subversive about this group was nothing to do with experiments with opium and free love: it was the fact that they dared to live lives of moral principle. They dared to take seriously those revolutionary concepts of liberty, equality and fraternity which the ruling class then, as now, has always found so terrifying. They weren't abstract ideas to them, they were active principles, well worth striving and fighting for.

'Don't give me that glorious war-record stuff,' said Hancock. 'McWhinnie was an office wallah. Sat out most of the war in Camberley, stamping dockets. No wonder. Fella's as bent as a Chinaman's elbow. They shifted him out east once with a load of other shirt-lifters; sent him to guard an ammo-dump in Burma.

Probably hoped the lot of 'em would get blown to kingdom come.'

Half a dozen of the conference members were crowded into a little attic room, high up in the Hurst's eaves. Hancock had managed to lay hands on some vodka, which he doled out in plastic cups – but, as keeper of the bottle, insisted on taking charge, posting sentries to warn of bandits approaching. In one corner Gibbon was telling Terry the superiority of what he called 'genuine research' over arty-farty theory. What he wouldn't give for the manuscript of the lost section of *Basque Cantoes*.

'Make it up,' said Danny joining them, having drunk a glass or two of vodka.

'Make it *up*?' said Gibbon slowly, feeling there must be a joke here, somewhere, which had passed him by.

'Sure. What difference would it make? It was his fiction, after all. Spies, revolution, informers. Why this fetishistic attachment to bits of paper?' Gibbon, unsure if this were some of the famous irony which tended to be lost on him, was temporarily taken aback. 'You don't seriously suggest fabricating evidence?' he said. Danny nodded.

'Why ever not?'

'Is that your idea of research?'

'Not really. I thought it might satisfy your own rigorous obsession with scraps of –' he raised his hand to signal speech-marks, inadvertently spilling his vodka, 'evidence.'

Gibbon shrugged and turned away saying it was impossible to argue with anyone who showed such a cavalier disregard for scholarship. Danny, unrepentant and fairly squiffy, helped himself to another vodka and demanded how many letters Gibbon would think he needed? One? Ten? A *hundred*? And what would they have to say? 'Let me see,' Danny put down his glass and took up a heroic stand. ' "I believe the people of England should arise and take up arms..." Something like that?'

Speaking now with a tone of barely concealed anger, Gibbon said he didn't share Danny's Stalinist disregard for facts. The others whooped with delight.

'Very overrated, facts,' said Danny, getting Hancock to fill his cup again. '*Never* spoil a good theory with too many facts.' He grinned.

He preferred fiction? – said Terry. He turned to face her.

Not fiction – he declared, and paused. *Criticism.* There were loud noises, as of toilets being flushed, but he went on. 'It's only prejudice which insists on seeing critics as a kind of –'

'Parasite?' said Gibbon.

'Not the word I would have chosen, but it will do. Parasites. It is only the truly defensive, unreflecting or *ignorant* writer who would regard the author of *Biographia Literaria* as a parasite.' There was another cheer. Danny, looking rather flushed, took a deep breath. 'The critic, truly regarded, is the only real creative artist.'

Hancock blew a loud raspberry.

'You can mock, but I mean it. The novelist's world is monotone; the critic makes it stereophonic. His world is infinite. The novelist toils away, ruthlessly paring down his imaginative range...'

'Or *her*,' said Terry.

Danny made a little bow. 'Of course,' he said, '*her* imaginative range. To produce what?' He raised his right hand with three fingers extended, which he proceeded to count off. 'One, consistency of character; two, coherence of plot; three, authenticity of tone. The novelist's creativity is essentially exclusive. The critic, by contrast, suffers no similar restrictions. To her,' (he bowed towards Terry) 'all things are possible. A critic takes a simple fictional object in a story, let us say...' he paused, and looked round the room. Hancock offered him the now empty bottle; Morris, rocking back and forth on his chair, leant forward to wave the curtain but, in doing so, lost his balance, came crashing to the floor and was greeted with another loud cheer. Danny turned, took up the fallen chair and waved it at them.

'...A chair,' he said. 'She may deconstruct it as a cultural myth, decode its Freudian significance, analyse its social status, assess its role in gender politics, translate, historicise it, dehistoricise it. Out of a simple chair a critic can develop a cultural investigation boundless in complex subtleties. But for a novelist it's just something to sit on.'

Hancock started a little ironic applause, but no one joined in. Morris, bruised by his fall, lay moaning on the floor.

'That's the marvellous thing about Madoc. Thanks to the critics, he has become a universal character. For Max, he's an authentic proletarian; for Gwendolen Glover he was Eternal Youth. There's a Madoc for Friends of the Earth, a Madoc for the Welsh Nats, even a bloody Madoc for the GCSE exam boards. It's got absolutely nothing to do with facts, manuscripts or letters.'

'How do you have the patience?' Alice sat in the corner window seat watching Gill execute neat strokes with two of the boldest in her set of calligraphic pens. That morning Gill had visited her publisher and been commissioned to produce a children's book on lovable Victorian secretaries, exploring the many styles of lettering.

'It's very restful,' said Gill, turning from a terse ironmonger's letter, to the much more ornate style of the Earl of Magnafold.

'Rather you than me. D'you want some tea?'

When Alice had gone Gill put down her pen. It would soon be time to move. The conference in Wales would have started now, so she could reoccupy her own house without any fear that Danny would return for at least a week. Carefully she washed the nibs under the corner tap. Now that she had a commission things would be different. She went downstairs and joined Alice in the kitchen where they talked about Jane's exhibition. Alice, who seemed not to have opinions of her own, liked to base her views on those of someone she knew and was delighted to join Gill in approving, with reservations, the paintings they had seen. Flicking through the exhibition catalogue, Gill admitted that she couldn't help liking them. Such bright, bold colours! If she knew where she was living she'd have bought one, she said, though rifling through she noted they seemed to start at £200.

'But you'll patch it up?'

Gill shrugged. 'I wonder who the young man was,' she said, looking at his jet black hair and torso muscles. 'Jane's latest?'

Alice, who had never particularly liked Danny (possibly because, at a drunken party years before, she had flung herself at him only to suffer the humiliation of being flung back), seemed to pluck up interest.

'You will, though?'

Gill smiled. 'I'll be moving out soon,' she said, bending down to pick up a bottle of vodka. 'Let's have a celebration.'

'Not an altogether bad brew,' said Hancock, who was examining the label on his empty vodka bottle. There had been a motion to adjourn when the vodka ran out but Morris, recovered from his bruise, volunteered the whisky in his room. Terry said she had had enough and left, accompanied by Danny, who went to phone Gill, convinced she would by now have reoccupied the flat. Whatever gave him that idea, or possessed him, at half-past midnight, to ring her, was a mystery to them all. Hancock tried to dissuade him, but it was no good. Danny was convinced she was there and went to use the payphone in reception, emptying his pockets of his change, which he arranged in charming patterns on the table. There was much trouble getting through to the number, and he rang the Welsh operator to get it for him. But when he got what she assured him was the number, there was no answer. He completely failed to understand what could have happened and tried again, but again the same thing happened. The phone just rang and rang. He slammed the phone down and went up to Terry's room, banging on the door. She was undressing and didn't come at once, but when she did she was wearing a japanese-style nightdress and the room smelt absolutely heavenly. He tried to tell her, through the partly opened door, that he knew it wasn't *his* room, but still he couldn't understand why she wouldn't open the door, just for a *minute*, to let him in just to explain. She said he was drunk, but he assured her, vehemently, that he was far from it. He just wanted to explain that he knew Gill was there; not *there,* he emphasised, meaning Terry's room – to which, by the bye, he would very much appreciate being invited in. Just to sit down and explain how he knew Gill *was there.* He perfectly appreciated that it was twelve o'clock, or one o'clock, was it? Well he would take her word for that, and would go away very soon, very soon indeed. That was a lovely smell. What was it? Was it really lavender? It was really gorgeous. Couldn't he just come in, just for a minute, just to sit down and explain. He was sorry – he didn't mean to touch her breast. No really, that hadn't been on his mind at all. He thought they were magnificent, by the way. He hoped she didn't mind him saying that? Did she? Because if she did, he wouldn't say it. Well, he wouldn't say it *again*. Even though they were. Truly magnificent. Just as breasts ought to be. All right. All right. Good night. Good...

'Tactically speaking old sport,' said Hancock, polishing off the last of a flask of whisky as Danny returned, 'I think you may have missed a trick there.'

5

Terry made sure she was down at the pool a good ten minutes early. The door of the old summer-house pavilion, usually kept locked, was left unfastened during daylight hours as a special concession to conference guests. She pushed it open and stepped inside. There were holes in the roof and the whole place smelt of damp, rotting wood, crumbling stonework and a general atmosphere of neglect. Here and there patches of creosote and the rusting cans of garden fertilizer added a sickly sweet chemical aroma of rich decay. In a corner an old croquet mallet leant up against a heavy roller; along the shelf lay a set of mildewed *Headway Histories,* with a picture of Napoleon on the cover. The place was mainly used now as a glorified garden-shed; seed-trays and window-box arrangements were piled across the floor and down one side of the whitewashed bench. Nothing much seemed to be growing, just a few fungi, livid orange and mould white; no doubt Morris could find some sort of coded message in them.

She didn't know if Danny would show up. He might choose to regard their arrangement as provisional – which her decision to spend part of the previous night talking to Gibbon had cancelled. Terry's instincts were very precise; she valued neatness highly and liked to place people in her mind. Danny was still a puzzle, with opinions on everything and belief in none of them. She flicked through the

pages of *The Last Nightingale* that she had brought
along as a possible guide. At least he was more interesting than Gibbon, whose beliefs, she had found,
began and ended with himself. She stepped outside,
into the sunlight, and saw him waiting at the far side
of the pool, pacing and looking at his watch.

'Hi!' she called across. He turned to look.

'You're late,' he said, sounding tetchy. 'I thought
you'd changed your mind. I've been here for ages.'

'So have I.'

'Where were you?'

'In the summer-house.'

'Oh. You didn't say the summer-house. You said the
pool.'

'Oh, did I? Sorry.'

She stood in front of him. His eyes looked tired. He
looked as if he hadn't slept.

'Isn't the water lovely?' she said, kneeling down and
letting it dribble through her fingers. 'I'd love to take
a dip.' She looked up at him, standing shadowed by
the sun. 'Wouldn't you?'

'Not many manuscripts in there.'

Overnight she had done much reading and formed
a conviction that the manuscripts, if they existed (she
strongly suspected they did), were to be found in one
of the Hurst's two towers. The so-called 'North', was
really a gatekeeper's residence, ruined and locked up
some three hundred yards along the Aberdovey Road:
the 'Main' was a perilously narrow clock tower, roped
off from conference guests, that ascended behind the

Llewellyn Building. Having come so far to make her discovery, Terry was determined on a thorough search of both. She stood up, drying her hand on a chestnut bough.

'You think this is a waste of time?'

'Did I say so?'

'You didn't have to. I don't care. I'll search for them anyway.'

'I'll keep you company,' he said.

'Don't strain yourself.'

'That's all right,' he said. 'We made a bet.'

Slowly they made their way through the alley of tall hedges towards the arboretum.

'I thought you'd found yourself a new helpmate.' He stooped to pick up a broken strand of hedge and swished it awkwardly before him.

'Oh,' she said, 'and who would that be?'

'Isn't this more Gibbon's sort of thing?'

Terry loved to hear the little angry tremor in his voice. He was jealous. She'd made him jealous. How easy men were to deal with, after all.

'His kind of thing?' she repeated, with just the tiniest hint of teasing.

'Searching through old ruins.'

'Oh no, not Max. He'd never do.' She reached the open meadow, turned and smiled at him. 'Imagine if we found something. Who d'you think would get the credit?'

'The North Tower of this once noble edifice, at the time of which we speak, was in that becoming state of partial dilapidation which visitors of an aesthetic sensibility were wont to pronounce "most picturesque". Such connoisseurs were no less charmed by the semi-ruination of its battlements, the mouldering masonry of its once proud turrets, embrasures and portals, than by the infestation of its galleries by colonies of ravens. Time, which makes mock of Man's attempts at immortality, had weathered down the cunning mason's ornamental stonework; and where once the lily and the rose had intertwined in sandstone around its high-arched casements, now only ivy spread its fragile tendrils. It happened, one still night, when the pale moon shone down on hawthorn, yew and cypress, that two strangers approached the tower...

'She's wrong about the trees,' said Danny, plucking a leaf from an overhanging bough of beech. 'That's oak, for certain.'

They stood some fifty yards from the dry moat which shelved down towards what remained of the North Tower, filled with refuse from the home-farm and now partially grassed over. Abandoned clumps of straw lay among nettles, dock-leaves, dandelions and poppies. The sun overhead was hot, but trees provided a pleasant shade. Danny took off his jacket, slung it across his shoulder and felt the sun warm upon his face. It was a day for picnicking under the trees, not scrabbling about in gloomy cellars.

'Over here,' said Terry, walking ahead, but Danny loitered in a glade watching swallows tumble overhead and eyeing rusty coils of barbed wire surrounding the base of the tower. Stern notices, in both English and Welsh warned 'DANGEROUS STRUCTURE – KEEP OUT!' but Terry paid them no heed. Her head and shoulders were visible as she clambered down the slope of the moat, her bright white blouse shimmering in a heat haze. Her voice sounded very distant, and lilting, like a child's.

'Here, I've found a gap.'

Danny went to the moat's edge, looked down and saw Terry, crouched down and crawling under the wire. A stray barb hooked at the hem of her skirt.

'Mind your clothes,' he called. She wore her blouse knotted in front over a short red skirt, with white briefs and stockings decorated with butterflies; hardly ideal for exploring. 'They'll tear!'

Terry waggled her rear at him and wriggled free. 'Easy,' she said. The sun was directly overhead and, looking up towards him, she had to shade her eyes.

'Isn't it locked?'

'Don't know.' She threw up her shoulders. 'Shouldn't think so. Who from?'

'Shouldn't you look?'

'Aren't you coming?'

Danny crawled his way crabwise down the slope, and stared at the hole in the wire.

'Through there?'

'Nothing to it.'

Danny shook his head. 'I don't think so,' he said.

'Lie flat and wriggle through.' Danny pointed to a pile of rabbit droppings. Terry made an impatient gesture with her arms.

'Lie sideways then.'

Danny flopped down and tried it sideways, squirming forward and leaning on his left elbow till he felt the wire snagging at his shirt.

'I'm stuck,' he said, as though proving something.

'Oh, Danny!' she yelled, exasperated. Eventually he was through.

'There,' she said. 'Easy, wasn't it?' Danny looked down at the smear of rabbit droppings down across his trouser leg. 'It'll wash,' she said.

As he had predicted, the door was locked.

'Now what?' he tried wiping the smudge from his trousers with a tissue, but only made it worse.

'What about those window things?'

'Embrasures.'

'Whatever.'

The embrasures were narrow, dangerous and at least six feet from the ground.

'Plenty footholds,' said Terry, demonstrating. The stonework promptly crumbled under her feet.

'Harder. I won't break.' Spreading his palms under Terry's buttocks, Danny felt a deliciously warm sensation. The muscles tensed. She had decided this was the only way. 'Now. Push!' she said, and Danny pushed.

Inside the tower was cool and dank, and Terry shivered in her flimsy summer clothes. Underfoot the sodden earth and broken flagstones were treacherous, with a slimy carpet of fungus. She slithered trying to reach out for the wall, but it was damp with mould and moss. Sunlight, filtering though the narrow aperture, was greenish; something cold crawled over her naked foot and made her shudder. She squirmed to get a grip.

'All right?' Danny, finding an orange-box further round the moat, climbed on it and peered inside. 'Phew, what a stink!'

Terry didn't reply, but beckoned him inside; he could just make out her pale hand circling in the darkness. There was something faintly ghostlike about the slender wrist and narrow fingers curling upwards in the gloom. Laboriously he hauled his knees up to the sill, jumped down inside, landing heavily, skidding on the fungus and toppling in slime.

'Jesus!'

Terry burst out laughing, her laughter echoing round the walls like water in a waterfall. Danny's leg was numb with pain.

'I think I may have broken something.' His voice reverberated round the dark chamber.

'Poor Danny.' Her words, meant sympathetically, became quite mocking with the echoes. 'Shh, listen…'

All Danny could hear was a silence so oppressive that he felt his stomach swimming with a kind of nausea. This place was an open catacomb, fetid and dank; his clothes hung clammily upon him, like grave clothes. It appeared his leg wasn't broken after all, only paralysed with a strange panic that beset him. Terry seemed almost in a trance, gliding airily, as if weightless, about this gloomy dungeon, brushing her pale arms against the walls.

'There's nothing here,' he said. 'I told you.'

'Listen.'

He tried listening but could hear nothing, he said.

'Exactly,' her eyes were like far-off torches in the dark, 'nothing. The silence. It's like a dream.' She held herself still and alert, like a field creature scenting danger.

'This is ridiculous!' As Danny's eyes grew more accustomed to the darkness, he spied a grey shape in the corner from which the worst smells seemed to come.

'What in heaven's name?'

Although inert, the surface of the object shimmered in the half-light with a faint luminescence. Moving closer he could just make out the shape of a head.

'Oh God!' He turned back, retching, to the embrasure, and held on to the rusty palings, gasping for air. It was a dead sheep, its decomposing head swarming with maggots.

'No wonder it stinks.'

'It's all right,' she whispered, 'it's just dead.'

Danny had had enough though, and pushed a heavy stone into position under the embrasure, uncovering as he did so another teeming colony of insects.

'Ugh! I'm getting out,' he hoisted himself up to the sill. 'Coming?' He held out his arm to help her up, but Terry's voice was still soft and trance-like.

'It's so peaceful,' she said.

'Suit yourself,' he said, then jumped down outside and breathed in lungfuls of warm fresh air.

Although known generally as 'brethren', a surprisingly large number of the Nightingale community were women or 'female brethren' – as they were called – a designation which none of them seemed to find the least bit odd. As secretary to the conference, Brother Jennifer was ubiquitous, perched in the front of every lecture with a line of biros in her pocket, a notepad on her lap. At the start of every session she would bound forward, apologise profusely, and read out a list of memos, pronouncing every item, however minor, with a histrionic flourish which was a sad loss to some amateur drama group. Regrettably – she would say and pause, beaming at them – it seemed that one or two of them had neglected to observe community rules. At first no one knew how to respond to this business of being reprimanded publicly, like naughty children. Only when it became clear that Brother Jennifer's kindergarten manner was accompanied by a genuine sense of fun did they relax and treat the whole thing as a very serious game. Their daily admonishments were ritualised into a form of set responses, led by Brother Jennifer.

'Two cigarette ends, in a tin on floor B of Perry Madoc!' she began, and the assembled company responded with a deeply serious, '*Oh!*' She would go on, raising her voice a touch: 'Four cigarette ends on a window sill of the Llewellyn lounge,' and the congregation (no other word was fitting) would answer, '*Ooh!*' Finally she would come to a climax treating every syllable with a separate breath: 'An emp-ty wine bot-tle behind a door of the Lle-wel-lyn lounge!' and the whole room responded with a rapturous, '*Oooh!*' She beamed at them for a moment. And now, she said, she looked forward to a truly splendid afternoon of lectures, and sat down to thunderous applause.

Having abandoned all thoughts of North Tower as a repository of manuscripts, Terry was anxious to investigate the Main. Danny was less enthusiastic. He was tired, he said, stretched out on his bed and holding up an arm to drag her down beside him. They'd done enough for one day, surely; what they needed was a little relaxation. It would make them bright and eager for tomorrow's research. But Terry wasn't listening, and neatly evaded his outstretched arm. Their time was limited, she said, standing behind his bed, pulling off her T-shirt and searching her suitcase for a replacement. He turned, placed his lips on hers and held her tight, which she submitted to for an instant, then pushed him back and looked at herself briskly in his mirror.

'Not now,' she said. 'God, my hair!'

'When then?' he said, slipping his hands down to caress her buttocks. She kissed him about as sensually as a hairdryer. 'Later,' she said, removing his hands. 'First we have to search Main Tower.'

The conference programme for the afternoon specified a discussion, chaired by the girl in spectacles, of Celtic druid lore in the *Basque Cantoes*, whose appeal was keen but limited. Most conference delegates had opted for the coach trip to Aberystwyth. Nobody enquired what Terry and Danny were doing when they slipped behind the cleaners' cupboards and, ignoring a large 'PRIVATE' notice, climbed up the staircase of Main Tower behind Llewellyn lounge. Up and up they went, till, at the third landing, the carpet gave out and some unstained markings in the middle of the stairway showed where it had been. A red-tasselled rope hung across the way with NO ENTRY on a gilt edged card hanging down.

'Are you sure we should be doing this?' said Danny.

'Go on,' she said, eyes bright, pushing him from behind. He lifted the rope and they climbed further. From this point on the stairway narrowed at every landing, tiny casements admitted the merest gleams of light, while underfoot the wood gave way to stone. The walls were unplastered and, in the darkness, Danny's elbows rubbed awkwardly against brick and lime. They climbed so far that, still groggy from his sleepless night, he lost count of the flights.

'How far have we come?' he said, leaning against the wall, taking deep breaths and using the feeble casement light to make out their position on the official conference hand-out. Terry pulled his arm.

'It can't be far now,' she said, overtaking him and climbing further, confident as a thief.

'We could do with a torch,' said Danny, stubbing his toe against the banister. They passed another embrasure, this one unglazed, and the chill air made them shiver. 'Can't be much further.' She squeezed his hand and remarked on a formidably learned article she had once consulted, suggesting that the tower of Prophylactus in the *Aesculapiad* was, like the tower of Babel, supposed to stretch up to infinity? Danny flushed with pleasure and missed his footing on the narrow, uneven stairs. 'When he had written that,' he said, rubbing his bruised shin, 'he'd been seated in a cosy library, using his imagination…'

At last they came to a door at an angle to the stairs, with a large old-fashioned iron knob and keyhole.

'Try it,' she said, stepping so close he could almost feel the warm scent on her neck and breasts. Their hands touched as he reached for the knob and pushed. Nothing. He tried it forwards and backwards, pushing hard. It didn't budge.

'Let me.' She grasped and pushed it, thrusting her whole weight behind it.

'It's locked,' he said.

'Wait,' she raised her skirt and took a credit card from the top of her tights. She was full of surprises. Squatting down she slid the edge of the card into the door-crack and eased it up and down.

'Try it now.'

He yanked the knob, pulling it to and fro while beneath him she prised at the catch. Nothing. The lock held fast.

'Damn it.'

Still crouched, her skirt hoisted to her waist as she fiddled with her card, and he sensed with pleasure the warm pressure of her thighs against his calf. As a matter of interest – he said – did she do this often?

'Only in the interests of research,' she answered, still wrestling with the thing. 'And, of course, professional advancement.'

'Of course.'

She flicked back a stray lock of hair which brushed against his wrist, and he looked down at it. Then he noticed something in the corner of his eye – a key suspended from the wall.

'As fun as all this is, why don't we use that?' he said, nodding in the appropriate direction.

She looked up, and there flickered across her face at first embarrassment, and then victory.

Inside the attic room was utter darkness. Just for a moment he felt a child's terror and drew back, panicky.

'What do you see?'

'Nothing,' he said, his lips dry.

'Damn! Do you have a light?'

He felt inside his pockets, awkwardly, not wanting to let go. When he found his matches he gingerly struck up, but his hands shook and the match blew out in a gust from the embrasure.

'Damn. I don't have many left.'

'Come here,' she whispered. He waited till he could make out her shape, smell her scent and feel her all around him. She cupped her hands cradling the flame as he lit up. At first he thought the match-light would die out, but gradually it rose and cast an eerie glow around the walls.

'Look.' She pointed to a candle, standing in a candlestick in the middle of a squat, old-fashioned table, with thick gouts of wax congealed along its sides like frozen leaves. Sheltering the guttering match between her hands, he lit the wick – the flame sputtered, nearly died, but then burnt brightly. The room they were in was small, lined all around with bookshelves and exuding an unmistakable odour of damp. Most of the shelves were empty, except those against the south wall. Going over, they began to pull down volumes which, old and damp, almost fell apart in their hands. Danny took down a *Vicar of Wakefield* and a *Rasselas*, both printed in the 1840s, while Terry uncovered a shelf of Latin Primers.

'From the, Hurst's time as a public school,' whispered Danny. He didn't know why he was whispering, but it seemed appropriate. He had an odd tingling of excitement in his stomach and an overpowering desire to kiss Terry here, in this Main Tower attic. He went over to where she was squatting, leafing through the books on the bottom shelf. 'They did enough Latin,' she said. 'Look at these: Suetonius, Tacitus, Caesar, Virgil.'

'*Timeo danaos et dona ferentes*,' he recited, bending down suddenly and kissing her on the mouth, which she allowed him to do, although her mind was elsewhere. She was convinced the *Basque Cantoes* were up here. But where? On the north wall the bookcase was empty. Feeling his way along the shelves, Danny severed the pin from the tail of the dovetail joint, and the whole structure started to crumble. 'Nothing here,' he said, feeling his way down the last, east bookcase. 'Time for a bath, I reckon. How about you?' Terry didn't answer, but went round the room again, north, south, east and west, still looking.

'Candle won't last much longer,' said Danny, standing by the door, anxious to leave and secretly rather pleased. He had always known there was nothing to find. Terry checked again the table, corners, bookcases. Down on the floor, at the foot of the west bookcase which also held Latin Primers, she noticed a bundle of papers which she'd assumed were only rubbish, like the bundle in the north corner. But she suddenly spotted they were tied up with black silk ribbon. Whoever ties up rubbish with black silk? As soon as she saw it, she knew. She screamed and clapped her hands so the sounds echoed round the walls. 'Over here,' she said in a hushed voice, 'there's something here!' But, as she said it, the candle guttered and died. Danny tried to relight it, but it was almost in darkness that she cautiously eased the bundle out of its hiding-place.

6

The continued absence of McWhinnie put the conference organisers in something of a fix. As undisputed elder statesman of Madoc studies, McWhinnie's name spread through the programme like a rash: McWhinnie to give the Llewellyn Lecture in the Owen Glendower Hall; McWhinnie to lead the toast to the immortal memory alongside the immortal pool (a ceremony which Carstairs thought quite tasteless); McWhinnie to chair the final Plenary Session of the conference in the Llewellyn lounge. From a casual reading of the programme it would appear the conference was devoted not to Madoc, but McWhinnie. But where was he? Repeated phone calls to Oxford proved fruitless; the porters hadn't seen him for days. A bundle of undergraduate essays in his pigeon-hole had lain undisturbed since May.

Grant Morris was understandably furious. As Conference Organiser, McWhinnie's disappearance cast a wholly unmerited slur on his abilities. He went round obsessively, insisting that *it wasn't his fault*. He had *two* letters from that blasted man (he waved them at anyone who asked), promising faithfully to be there. Carstairs found it equally irksome. As nearest to McWhinnie in seniority and status, he found himself elevated into a most unwelcome eminence. In the interests of general harmony, it was he who was persuaded to go through the programme, ticking off the items where he might be prevailed upon to step into the breach. The toast was no problem. Carstairs was happy to propose the toast, although it did occur to him to wonder whether it were something less than honorific to propose *anybody's* immortal memory in the non-alcoholic muck they proposed to serve. Morris promised to look into the possibilities of procuring a more appropriate beverage. About the Plenary Session, Carstairs was far less sanguine. Really he had not kept up with all the most recent stuff. Surely there must be someone else. But, Morris argued, what was required was someone more detached, above the hurly-burly, to act as referee. Carstairs said he must remember to bring a whistle. The Llewellyn lecture was a wholly different matter. Carstairs was just beginning to point out that he really couldn't take on something of that nature, when, to his chagrin, Morris took him at his word without even the pretence of dissuasion.

'Of course, of course,' he said, 'that would be *too* much to expect.'

There was something about his manner that grated with Carstairs. In spite of his punctilious politeness – or possibly because of it – the man's intellectual arrogance was too apparent. It showed in his cultivated deference towards academic seniors whom he despised. It was a moment's blissful inspiration, for Carstairs to let slip, as he stood up to leave and went hunting round the room for his old tweed cap, the thought that McWhinnie's Chair at Oxford would soon be vacant. Naturally Morris was too sharp to be taken in by the old codger pose. Unless he was very much mistaken, he had just received a pretty clear indication of Carstair's mind. The two men parted (after Carstairs retrieved the cap that he'd been sitting on) privately congratulating themselves on the secret intelligence that had passed between them. It was astonishing how easily the rumour spread. Within hours it was the subject of general gossip. Vastly amused at the mischief thus provoked, Carstairs did his best to promote the atmosphere of rivalry by judicious indiscretions to other hopefuls. As the supposed dispenser of academic patronage, he found himself enjoying a pleasantly enhanced status. His words were hung on as never before, his little jokes greeted with gales of laughter, and he rediscovered a skill, grown rusty with disuse, of delivering coy phrases of delphic ambiguity which had the power to curl up the hearer's toes with pleasure.

'Of course,' said Danny, 'they can't be genuine.' He and Terry made their way across campus, overhearing the murmur of the Celtic seminar going on in the Llewellyn lounge. They took the stairs up to his room and, once inside, he went immediately to his suitcase hiding-place for his bottle of whisky. That whole set-up – he poured out two large measures and passed her one – it must have struck her. 'There's water in the tap. It's about the only thing they don't ration.' He slumped down in the armchair.

I mean, what more could she ask for? Cobwebby old books, wax-encrusted old candle, and then, neatly *un*hidden underneath a dusty old shelf!...

Terry neatly kicked off her shoes and drew up her feet to sit cross-legged on the bed, from where she began, very carefully, to undo the bundle of papers. Outside the attic they looked smaller, older, more frail than when she had first espied them.

'Maybe.'

Slowly she undid the bundle, whose outer sheets, she found, were made up from the *North Wales Mercury* of April 1847. Inside these were much more fragile scraps of manuscript, which she spread out with care, one by one, across the counterpane. Danny leant over and picked up a torn piece, like a square of toilet tissue, written all over in a crabbed sepia scrawl.

'Even the paper,' he said, holding it up to the light.

'Careful!' Terry cupped another tiny scrawled leaf in her hands and studied it intently. Just holding it gave her a thrill.

'I don't know.' She tipped her head to one side, and Danny watched the slow rise and fall of her blouse. 'I think you're wrong. To me they look gen*yuwine* enough.' She gave the word an artificial twang.

'Come off it,' he said, flapping the piece he'd picked up in front of her. 'It's a trick. Not even a very good one. Look at the handwriting. That's never Madoc's.'

He made a grab for the McWhinnie edition lying on the shelf, which had a frontispiece photograph of the begging letter sent by Madoc a week before he died.

He placed the piece of manuscript beside it. 'There, look,' he said, 'not like it at all. *I* could do better than that.'

There was a pause.

'That's probably because he didn't write it,' Terry said, very calmly.

'Exactly!'

Terry smiled, sipped her whisky and played with the tassles of the lilac counterpane with her trailing hand.

'Jane did.'

'*What?*'

This time it was Terry who picked up the book and thumbed through the pages till she found an illustration of a page from Jane's *Diary*.

'Look!'

Danny looked. There was undoubtedly a marked similarity.

'It's in the way she crosses her t's, and the d's, the loop of her d's…'

'That's ridiculous.'

'No, it's the truth. I think it's clearly Jane's hand.' Danny stood up, stared out of the window and was obviously annoyed. 'Naturally we'll have to have tests done, on the paper and the ink.' Terry went on.

'Naturally,' he said in a dismissive voice.

'But don't you see? This can be very big. I don't see what you've got against it. It's our joint discovery. We sign up with a publisher to bring out *our* definitive edition. Jane Madoc's *Basque Cantoes* edited by Terry Franks and Danny Steele.'

'Now look,' he said, turning on her.

'OK, Danny Steele and Terry Franks. I don't care. Putting the woman first is pretty cheesy anyway. I reckon we should stick out for 3% each. Minimum. Should be a gigantic seller. Might get a Pulitzer or anything.' Terry began humming *Can't Buy Me Love*.

'You're not serious?'

'Sure. Why not? It's what they're gagging for. Madoc's stuff was written by his sister Jane. Fantastic...'

'And if you're wrong?'

Terry looked him full in the face. 'But I'm not,' she said, quite calmly, and Danny knew she meant it. 'Look, I'll admit that when I came to this conference I was looking for a book to write. On Madoc, his father, the bards, anything. But this!'

'But if they're fakes,' he said.

'What d'you mean, *fakes*?'

'I mean, they were just lying there. Waiting there to be found. I mean, McWhinnie's been over this territory for the past twenty years. You don't think *he'd* have found them?'

Terry didn't answer.

'Well?'

'What?'

'Doesn't it strike you as suspicious?'

Terry shrugged her shoulders. 'Perhaps. Like I say, I'll get them checked out. But I can feel it now. Oh, it's good.' She rose from the bed, shook out her hair and put her hand upon his arm. 'Now, *what* was it you were wanting?' She breathed softly, and her voice became instantly lascivious. Danny shook his arm free, feeling annoyed and cheated at the same time. It was a trick, he knew, but exactly how and why he couldn't tell. He stood up and moved to the door, looking at his watch. 'I don't know about you,' he said, 'but I want my tea.'

'There's just so much of the damn stuff published now,' said Hancock, twirling through the pages of a publisher's catalogue in weary disdain. 'There used to be a certain distinction about being a "Writer".' He framed the word in the air above his head. 'But *now* –' He let the catalogue slide to the floor. 'Could there honestly be,' he said in mock credulity, 'a market for *A Universal Guide to Gay Lyrics* or *Seventeenth Century School Rolls*?' He didn't enquire whether there was anything to be *gained* from reading tripe like that. He had long ago abandoned the idea that there was any point in reading books. Perfectly useless – that was their essential charm. He'd given up reading *new* books altogether. Someone, he couldn't remember who, had recommended he read a novel by some Jewish chap. Turned out to be all about wanking. 'Whacking-off' he called it. Summed up modern literature perfectly. 'Do you,' he turned to Danny, who had turned up at teatime and remained, 'ever actually *read*?'

Danny shrugged. 'From time to time,' he said. Hancock nodded philosophically.

'In the line of business, I suppose. Good luck to you. I'm not in the business any more. Promotion and so on. Got out of that particular rat race years ago. I said to myself, Clive, you are not a rat, so why get in the rat race. I say, do you see any of the goons about? I rather fancy another snifter.'

Stepping across the landing to the gents, Danny ran into Morris standing at one of the washbasins, flicking his hair into a quiff. His collar was open and he was loosening his tie, twisting it this way and that so it hung at a careless angle.

'I hear congratulations are in order…'

'What?' Morris dropped his comb and it clattered in the basin.

'No need to be coy.' Danny's voice echoed strangely off the green ceramic tiles. 'Word of advice though. Beware of Samuelbum. Rather miffed, I hear.' There was a hiss, and spurts of water washed down the urinal's glazed front. 'So, it's drinks all round?'

Morris slipped on his dark glasses. 'There's nothing definite,' he said, as though trying to convince himself.

'That's not what I hear.'

Back in the lounge they formed themselves into a little party.

'Count me in,' said Hancock, getting wind of a decent jar. Just then the doors opened and Samuelson walked in, but it was a version of Samuelson that Danny hadn't seen before. Peeled from his grey suit, he appeared like a crustacean without its shell –

pulpy, fleshy, pink. He wore a loose Hawaian shirt of violent orange and greens that flapped around him like a tent. On his legs were shorts of baggy khaki that sagged from his waist and creased around the crotch. At his side was the Buchanan girl, dressed in tennis gear and dripping with sweat.

'Been having a knock-up,' she exclaimed, wiping glistening beads of perspiration from her forehead and neck. Her body gave off the most exhilarating aroma of sweat, *ambre solaire* and sex.

'I thrashed her,' said Samuelson, eyes gleaming, 'I wiped the floor with her.'

'Rats! That last ball was out.'

'It was an ace, my dear. You were beaten by an ace!' Samuelson wiped his clammy palm across her rear.

'Just in time,' said Danny, explaining about Morris' rumoured elevation. It was wonderful to see the spasm of envy on Samuelson's face.

'O wow, real booze!' said the Buchanan girl removing her bright red headband and shaking out her blonde hair. She was panting from her exertions and against her damp white cotton blouse her nipples were visibly erect.

'There's really nothing definite,' said Morris.

'Get a move on,' said Hancock, 'last one there buys the drinks.'

Morris drove a white Golf, but Samuelson's car was a lurid green Capri with white-walled tyres, customised bumpers, confederate stickers and nylon leopard-skin seats. Two furry dice in day-glo pink hung at the windscreen. He got really narked when the Buchanan girl jumped in the back of the Golf.

'Suit yourself,' he sulked. Reluctantly Danny got in beside him, clearing a space amid Kentucky Fried Chicken cartons.

'On your marks.'

'Look at those tits,' said Samuelson, revving his engine till it screamed, 'have you ever seen tits like them?'

'Go!'

Samuelson slammed into first gear and there was a terrible crunch as it failed to engage. The Golf sailed past them, the Buchanan girl treating them to a regal wave.

'Bastard,' yelled Samuelson. 'We'll show 'em.'

He lurched from the main road down a sort of cart-track to the left, the car bouncing and jolting in deep ruts, throwing Danny forward, banging his head against the leopard-skin sun visor as the seat belts didn't work. 'Hang on,' said Samuelson, 'gets pretty bumpy ahead.'

They swerved between high hedges with the needle on fifty. Danny hated to think what would happen if they met anything coming the other way.

'Has he really got the Oxford Chair? Nasty little shit,' said Samuelson above the clatter of the engine.

'No chance.'

'What?' The car slowed a fraction.

'It's just a wind-up.'

'*What?*'

'Carstairs was winding him up.'

Samuelson looked round with an enormous grin on his face and the car almost collided with a tree stump.

'Sly old bugger.'

'Don't tell anyone. Least of all, Morris.'

'The sly old bugger.'

Danny ducked as he saw an overhanging branch swing out before them but somehow they passed underneath.

'By rights,' said Danny, 'I'd have thought you were the obvious candidate.'

'Too right,' said Samuelson vigorously, 'which doesn't mean I'll get it. I lack that little shit's supreme qualification: utter mediocrity.'

Suddenly they were in Victorian backstreets with a stagnant canal, a soap factory and rows of slate-roofed artisan villas whizzing past.

'And that little blonde tart. I really thought I was in there.'

Perhaps, Danny suggested, he had been too modest for his own good.

'Think so?'

'Doesn't do to be too modest. With women especially.'

'You could be right. Always has been my trouble.'

They raced under a low bridge covered with Welsh Nat graffiti, past a breaker's yard full of mangled agricultural machinery.

'Quite frankly it's all something of a dead loss on

the crumpet front. You seem to have bagged the only decent-looking bit of totty. I could have been in New York – hang on!' The car took a violent swerve to the right. 'I blame all this bloody feminism. 1982, that was the year. The Milton conference in Santa Monica. I bonked two structuralists in one afternoon – *and* gave a fantastic paper on *Paradise Lost*. You're right. Too bloody modest, that's my trouble.'

They made it to the pub a full minute before the others got there.

'What kept you?' shouted Samuelson, bellowing in the window as Morris was trying to park. 'Come on. It's practically last orders. Some of us are dying of thirst.'

Morris played the part of a good loser.

'By all accounts,' he said, 'the local brew packs quite a punch.' Samuelson stared contemptuously at the label.

'Piss,' he pronounced loudly, ordering some Germanic-sounding lager. The Buchanan girl had spritzer; Danny and Hancock stuck to Bass. Only Morris was tempted to sample what he insisted on calling the 'vin du pays'.

'Congratulations, professor!' said Samuelson, raising his glass.

'Oh, look… well, there's nothing definite.'

'Nonsense,' said Samuelson, with a knowing look to Dan, 'it doesn't do to be too modest. *Salut*!'

The corner jukebox pumped out a medley of oldies, including the Beatles' *I Wanna Hold Your Hand*.

'Brings it all back,' said Dan, 'Nineteen sixty-three. Wimbledon Palais. The Beatles' first No 1.'

'I thought that was *She Loves You*,' said Morris.

'Bollocks,' said Samuelson, 'it was *Love Me Do*,' starting into his own version of the track. Morris said he was sorry, but he had a distict memory of *Love Me Do* being beaten to the top by Gerry and the Pacemakers.

'Lay you any money you like,' said Samuelson.

Immediately they were locked in competition. For Samuelson no detail was too trivial, no record too ephemeral for him to lavish on it an extraordinary and incongruous display of erudition. Edging forward in his seat, fidgeting with his beer mat, twirling and untwirling wisps of his thick, black beard. Had he not achieved notoriety for publishing a comparison between the linguistic registers of Madoc and Jimi Hendrix? Apparently, during his year as Buckmaster Fellow at LA he had contributed a regular column to *Rolling Stone* on the troubadour roots of West Coast bands, and his collection of bootleg tapes – he liked to think – must be among the best in the country.

Hancock said that, music-wise, he didn't care for much after George Formby, and went to get another round. Actually, he said, when he got back, he didn't care for much before George Formby either; for him George Formby represented the peak of musical achievement. The Buchanan girl had never heard of George Formby. Hancock did a rendition, for her benefit, of *With My Little Ukelele In My Hand*, after which she couldn't stop laughing. It was the most obscene song she'd ever heard, she said, and asked him to do it again.

'Any money you like.'

Samuelson felt for the leather pouch he carried on his shoulder strap, pulled it out and slapped down a £20 note. Morris said he thought twenty pounds rather excessive.

'What would you prefer, *professor*? 20p?' He leered at him. '*5p*?'

Morris suggested a pound might be appropriate.

'*A pound*?'

Morris could see them all grinning.

'Sure you can spare it, *professor*?'

The amount wasn't the important thing – said Morris – it was the principle that mattered.

'Sure, sure,' said Samuelson, who thought they just had time for one more round. Morris said they should be getting back.

Don't worry, *professor*,' said Samuelson, 'I'll get yours. I can tell you're strapped for cash.'

'I thought you were driving?'

'Don't worry about me, *professor*. I drive best with a few beers inside me. Steadies the old nerves. There –' he held his arms in front of him, 'like a rock. Not a tremor. Not a twitch.'

When he'd had another pint, Samuelson suddenly confessed to feeling rather wobbly. Maybe Danny should drive his Capri back, Morris suggested, but Samuelson shook his head.

'No way. I'm not letting that little *deconstructionist* get his hands on my wheel. Here –' he tossed his carkeys to the Buchanan girl, 'you'll see me safely home dear, won't you?' She looked quite alarmed.

'Oh no, really, I couldn't.'

'Nonsense, you'll be fine.'

'But I've only ever driven a mini before.'

'Nothing to it. Drives like a dream. You'll like the feel of something bigger.' He leered at her. 'Goodness, is that the time? We really must be going. I'm due to lecture at four. Mustn't keep the punters waiting, eh, *professor*? I'm sure I'll be perfectly safe in your hands.' And, ignoring her protests, he drew her towards the door.

'A fiver says he doesn't make it,' said Hancock, after they had disappeared.

'Make what?' said Danny, 'the lecture?'

'That too,' said Hancock.

7

Carstairs took out his hip flask and poured himself another gin. By now the absence of tonic and the ugly taste of plastic no longer troubled him. In the general scheme of events they were minor inconveniences. By contrast, the whole McWhinnie thing was getting past a joke. The question no longer seemed to be when the wretched man would show up, but whether he would put in an appearance at all. All of which, to Carstairs' mind, was a pretty poor show. McWhinnie it was who had cast his lugubrious shadow over Madoc studies for nigh on thirty years; the least he could do was show up. There was an urgent tapping on the glass of the French windows opposite. Looking up, he saw a small dark face pressed against the pane. The features were sharp and direct, the eyes narrowly squinting and, with an uneasy feeling, he sensed he knew the face from somewhere but couldn't for the life of him say where. Then the tapping began again, tiny knuckles rapping hard against the pane. For a moment Carstairs hoped these signals, and the urgent beckoning gestures they made, were intended for someone else; but, apart from him, the Llewellyn lounge was quite deserted. Irritated, he stood up, went over and unlocked the door.

'Oh good. So glad I caught you.' It was Miss Powell-Davies, who tumbled into the room like a flock of gulls, arms flapping, green mac billowing out behind her. Dimly Carstairs wondered why all this woman's movements had to be so abrupt. She spoke non-stop, like a recorded message, putting him in mind of a diesel locomotive. Terrible embarrassment. Complete misunderstanding. Abject apologies. Seen the complete catalogue. One of those modern micro-thingummy machines. Could never get the hang of them. What was wrong with the old card-index? Anyway, there it was. Practically the whole shelf. *The Professor Carstairs*. She didn't know what to say. Powell-Davies plunged her hand into her mac pocket and pulled out two maps; Carstairs nodded and accepted them graciously. Whereupon Powell-Davies felt inside another of her capacious pockets and produced a brand new hardback copy of *Madoc, the Year of Making*. She held open the blank flyleaf and pushed it towards him. Her name, she blushed, was Penelope.

Of course. Carstairs' graciousness now swelled to a pleasurable magnanimity as he waved her to an armchair while he rested the book upon a table. *To Penelope*, he wrote – and hesitated, his pen hovering in the air. An embarrassed confusion of feelings fluttered across Powell-Davies' face as she fidgeted with the pleats in her long tartan skirt. Last one in the shop. Been all the way to Newport to get it. She'd been going there on council business anyway, but the librarian in Newport spoke of it so warmly. Really praised it to the skies. And after she had made such a prize ass of herself! *With warm regards*, wrote Carstairs, feeling now quite mellow and gallant, signing his name with a flourish: *Hugo Carstairs*. She had had an uncle Hugo. Used to take her riding on the downs above Plynlimon Bay. Powell-Davies gazed at the inscription with obvious pleasure and there was a silence. They both felt suddenly awkward, and Powell-Davies closed the book quite guiltily. Carstairs rather fancied another nip of gin but didn't like to risk it in front of this new admirer. He would gladly have offered her one, but somehow the hip flask and the plastic cups weren't quite the things. She looked up as if she was reading his mind.

'Temperance fanatics, aren't they,' she said, with obvious disapproval. Carstairs smirked. Evidently a game old bird. He slid the hip flask out of his side pocket.

'We have ways,' he said.

'Good man,' said Powell-Davies, resuming her county tones. He yanked another plastic cup from the wall dispenser by the drinking fountain and poured her a generous measure.

'Chin-chin,' she said, evidently untroubled by the notion of drinking it neat.

'Bottoms up,' said Carstairs, giving her what he thought of as a roguish grin.

In the circumstances it was something of a surprise, not to say a miracle, when Samuelson turned up, exactly on time, to give his lecture. There he was, in the Llewellyn lounge at three o'clock, not exactly soberly or smartly dressed, but at least in his usual kit of rumpled suit, suede shoes, with a cricket-club tie knotted tightly beneath his chin. His step, as he strode towards the lectern, was only barely unsteady, and the slight slurring of his speech became not an impediment but an ornament of a lecture rich in rhetorical effects. Samuelson had perfected a technique of making his words at once impressive and totally unmemorable; his lectures had an automatic quality, well adapted to alcoholic delivery, in which his favourite words, *curiously* and *strangely*, occurred like bookends, to bolster up the verbiage in between. Scarcely a sentence that he uttered was free of either – sometimes both. *Curiously* he would say at the beginning of a sentence, going on to tease the audience with some syncopation of *light* and *sight,* or *might* and *right*; before tailing off into a *strange* downbeat murmur. All Samuelson's lectures seemed the same to Danny; the same soporific see-saw rhythm, balancing the *curiously effective* with the *strangely affective;* the same heavy-footed verbal somersaults, tumbling *eminence* into *immanence* or *conversion* into *conversation.* He looked round the room but *strangely* the Buchanan girl was nowhere to be seen – she was *curiously* absent. His gaze drifted up above Samuelson's head to where the sun's rays cast a *curious* slating light across the moulded busts of apothecaries and physicians, *strangely* reshaping their physiognomies with shadows.

To say Danny was surprised when Terry came bursting into his room would be a serious understatement. Their last encounter had seemed to put an end to any further thoughts of intimacy. Her manner conceded nothing. Giving a brisk peremptory knock, she pushed open the door, not waiting for a reply.

'This is an unexpected pleasure,' he said, getting up from the bed where he'd been leafing through his copy of the *Guardian*. 'I thought, as a male chauvinist, I was utterly forsaken.'

'Don't flatter yourself. Just for the moment it's your prime attraction,' said Terry, standing with her elbows jutting out like pistons to partially hide the Buchanan girl, who hovered behind her in the doorway. 'You're getting one last chance to redeem yourself.' Danny wasn't sure he liked the sound of that.

'Do I need it?' he said, adding that it made him sound like something left in a pawnshop.

'We need your help,' said the Buchanan girl, stepping forward.

'Oh! that's different,' said Danny, offering her a chair and closing the door. 'If it's a *favour* you want.' His choice of words made Terry frown, and he was conscious she was making a definite effort *not* to argue.

'It's about Samuelson,' said Buchanan looking white-faced.

'Samuelson?'

'I guess you've heard all about it!' Terry exploded. 'It's no laughing matter!'

'I guess there is a funny side,' the Buchanan girl conceded, running her hands through her hair. Her face was pale, eyes red from crying – and when, unconsciously, she thrust out her breasts, she seemed terribly young and girlish, behaving like a teenager.

'Babs!'

'I mean, *now* it's more ridiculous than scary' – she looked up at Dan – 'but at the time…'

'Of course,' he said, looking away and praying he wouldn't smile.

'He was *so* drunk.'

'Thank God for that!' said Terry, throwing up her arms and eyeing Danny closely.

'He got his thing…'

'His *penis*,' said Terry icily.

'He got it caught in his zip.' The Buchanan girl began to shake. She was sniggering and shuddering at once. 'You should have heard him yell!'

'That's not the point!' said Terry.

'When at last he got it free, it was so *small*!'

She giggled uncontrollably, and Danny sensed something desperate and – dared one use the word? – *hysterical* about the way her body shook. Suddenly her giggles turned to sobs and she started retching, holding her sides and gulping down lungfuls of air. Terry put her arm around her and tried to calm her.

'The bastard,' she said. 'It's so typical.'

Samuelson had got the Buchanan girl to pull off at a lay-by, saying he needed an urgent leak. Then he'd undone his trousers and made all sorts of extravagant promises about the references he'd write for her etc. Luckily they were quite close to the Hurst.

'I suppose I was expecting something,' said Babs, taking deep breaths. 'He kept wanting me to stop the car. I got as near back here as I could.'

'We're going to teach that bastard a lesson,' said Terry, and Danny couldn't but be struck that she seemed far keener on revenge than concerned for the victim of the assault. The two women had worked out their campaign in intricate detail. Step one was *The Letter*. At Terry's dictation the Buchanan girl had written him a simpering note, saying what a fool she'd been, behaving like a silly schoolgirl, how really sorry she was for making all that fuss, and that if he would meet her by the pool at midnight, she said, she would make it up.

'Should do the trick,' said Terry. Babs Buchanan wondered about adding a row of xxxs after her girlish signature, but didn't want him to be suspicious.

'Shove them in,' said Terry, 'with men it never does to be too subtle.' She turned to Danny. ' Your job is to make sure the bastard gets this, OK?' Danny said he didn't know if he was right for playing Cupid. Terry made a face. 'Don't worry,' she said, 'this is just the start.'

In the recreation room Hancock and Mitchell were laying bets on the nubility of the female Brethren. Hickson lolled back in an armchair, feet up on the stained coffee table, recovering from the thrashing Samuelson had just administered to him at ping-pong. Hickson took his defeat, 21–5, philosophically. After a while, the only pleasure of competing with Samuelson was the fascination of observing the ferocity with which he totted up these minor triumphs. No victory could be too complete. The loss of a single point was a mortification which caused him visible distress. Hancock had Brother Jasmine, the head gardener, as clear favourite. They watched her at work in the Dean's garden, pinning back wisteria against the chapel wall. According to common-room consensus, they weren't hot pants she was wearing – not tight enough across her rear to be proper hot pants.

'Warm-pants?' suggested Mitchell. You could see they didn't stretch smoothly down the curve of her buttocks; they flapped against her...

'Thighs?'

'Loins?'

'God, this place is frustrating,' said Hancock, flopping on the sofa. At which point Danny came in with the letter for Samuelson.

'Found this in your pigeon-hole,' he said, tossing it across the ping-pong table to Samuelson, who was wiping his forehead with a towel. His colour changed as soon as he saw the writing and he quickly opened it.

'Not bad news, I hope,' said Danny. Samuelson smirked but tried to hide it.

'No no, it's nothing special,' he said, making a rotten job of concealing his elation. Hancock snatched up the envelope and sniffed.

'A woman?' he enquired, but Samuelson went on wiping his face.

'It's nothing,' he said, making sure to shove the letter in his pocket before the others could get a sight. 'Which of you dozy buggers fancies another game?'

As far as the official programme was concerned, Terry was aware her role was to be a stop gap between McWhinnie and lunch. How she got on the official programme was something of a mystery, until Morris confided there had been no rush of takers to share the session with such an obvious star-turn. Now, in McWhinnie's continued absence, her time was lengthened from twenty minutes to half an hour. She felt nervous, yet fully confident that she would provide those who attended with plenty to think about.

'You may have noticed,' she began, 'that I offer no title for this paper. This is not due to laziness or coyness. It is quite deliberate. It is…' – she paused – 'political. All there was on the programme for this lecture was my name, Terry Franks, and even that is false. A woman's name always is: it is a negotiable commodity, traded, before she is born, between powers that are, or will be, significant to her. She goes through her life branded and ticketed with men's names: her father's name, her husband's name –' she paused and took a sip of water. Her hands trembled, but she managed to keep nervousness out of her voice, though she was aware of Samuelson, watching and sneering at her.

'Obviously Jane Madoc,' she went on, 'like most women of that era, was limited in her opportunities for self-expression. Yet it would be naive and politically irresponsible to assume that women of her time cheerfully acquiesced with the strategies of male dominion that relegated them to domestic chattels, mistresses or pets. Their resistance had to be clandestine, often coded, always undercover; but the evidence of resistance was clear enough for those' – she looked round – 'with the patience and the willingness to see it. Jane Madoc's case was perfect. It was commonly accepted on the evidence of the three of them – Madoc, Jane Madoc and Williams – that it was Jane who "held the pen"' – she made little speech-marks in the air – 'during their poetic sessions. That much has never been disputed. Williams says in one letter, "and dear Jane held the pen", giving her a little pat on the head. Several surviving manuscripts are clearly written in her hand. What was, and always has been, a matter of dispute, was what his patronising phrase "held the pen" amounted to. Read conventional explanations – Gibbard in '56, Gwendolyn Glover in '63, McWhinnie in '72 – and they all present Jane very much in the role of faithful secretary, recording every word uttered by her male "bosses", transcribing them in a neat feminine hand. This seemed entirely natural to them; it never occurred to them to question a model which conformed exactly to their understanding of the way things are.' She paused, took a sip of water and gave a cool stare in the direction of Samuelson who, ostentatiously, leafing through a magazine, nevertheless shifted awkwardly in his seat. She pushed back her hair, took a deep breath, and carried on.

'It was damn near impossible to get a true fix on Jane. She's become so much a part of the accepted, acceptable conservative myth of' – her fingers went up – '"the Nightingale Group" as "divine Jane", Jane "the muse", etc. This hackneyed vocabulary of mock-adoration has had its customary effect in absorbing her. Under the guise of elevating Jane to a deity, it has reduced her to a household pet, almost part of the Nightingale furniture. Her imagination and ideas have been relegated – in the most civilised way of course – to a form of domestic support. Jane held the pen. The minds of the men are frequently likened by nineteenth-century critics to volcanoes, pouring forth molten streams of ideas in their creative torrent. But Jane? She was altogether quieter and more genteel – a reservoir, a harbour – she was woman as container: keeping what was valuable, the writing, safe and secure. But let us look a little more closely at what this entailed. Let us take a story like the Maria episode from Canto IV of the *Basque Cantoes*. Here we have a young girl, a maid, who comes to town at carnival time under the supposed protection of her kinsman, judge Claudius. Only Claudius isn't entirely what he seems. Instead of protecting her, he gets her drunk; and in place of taking her to church, in his carriage, he conveys her to the Forest of Carnal Desires. There, suddenly, in the dead of night, the manuscript ends. Instead of seduction, we have silence; instead of a rape, we have rupture, a blank, a gap in the text.' She paused and looked across at Samuelson. 'Or, that is what we had, until now!'

Slowly turning back to face the Hall, she picked up the slim leather folder from the desk before her, unzipped it with a single action and withdrew from inside a clear plastic file. Inside were the xeroxes of a dozen or so fragmentary manuscripts.

Now, at last – she said – she could reveal the ending of that story. But more significantly than that, what she had discovered would, without doubt, utterly and irrevocably transform ideas about the Nightingale Group itself. For the manuscripts were written entirely in Jane's hand, with Jane's own revisions, cancellations and annotations. They offered conclusive proof that she hadn't merely copied out the *Basque Cantoes* – she had conceived the poem, composed the poem, and was in fact the author of the *Basque Cantoes*!

When she finished, there was an awkward silence. Terry was high with nervous excitement, eager to deal with questions, her hand trembling as she poured out some water and took a sip. The next moment she was gripped by a terrible anticlimax. What if there weren't any questions? What if they hadn't taken in what she was saying? She was about to speak again, desperate to goad them into some response, when Gibbon raised his hand.

'I don't wish to seem obtuse,' he said, 'but I'm afraid it wasn't entirely clear, to me at any rate, what point you're making. I'd like to say that it was a magnificent paper,' (muttered *'Hear hears'* at that) 'but I am right, am I? I mean you're not speaking *literally*? You haven't literally discovered a new manuscript? It's more a kind of feminist conceit? Or have I missed the point entirely?'

Terry was afraid he had rather missed the point, or (tactfully) part of it. She had been talking entirely literally. The manuscripts were quite real. Returning to her leather folder she removed a file of xerox copies which she passed among them. She had already sent the originals to the labs at Bristol for scientific analysis, to establish beyond doubt their dating and so on. With such a major discovery as this, one had to be on the safe side. Samuelson cleared his throat and said that Dr Gibbon was sadly out of date if he assumed this kind of feminist delusion was designed merely for amusement. Nowadays the lady deconstructionists (what a revealing term that was!) were using real semtex. Now they were *literally* rewriting the stuff. In ten years time he rather doubted if there would be a single book left in the literary canon that was acknowledged to be written by a man. Or if there were they certainly wouldn't be studied in universities. After Jane Madoc, what? Wilma Shakespeare? Carol Dickens?

That stirred them up. Terry was almost grateful to Samuelson for reacting so perfectly to type. She was careful, though, to remain very much on her dignity, remarking that it was sadly characteristic of some male academics, when confronted by the serious researches of their feminist colleagues, to retreat behind a barrage of prejudices, rather than evaluate the evidence placed before them.

'Examine closely, if you will,' she said, 'the imagery. The sword which sinks upright into the lake is of course a symbolic representation of the male sexual organ absorbed into the female. It is, in fact, an evocation of the annihilation of the masculine. The pen may be the penis but it is not *actually* the pen which marks the virgin page, but ink, which is dark, fluid and female – formless itself yet giving form to everything – mysterious as blood.'

Other responses were predictably mixed. It was generally agreed the hand was very like Jane's, not the formal 'fair-copy' hand with which they were all familiar, but a rough, impressionistic, often negligent hand, full of abbreviations, contractions and revisions. All of which might, Carstairs surmised, be said to represent the febrile imagination at work. This partial endorsement, from such an unlikely source, was pure delight. Frankly Carstairs was the last person Terry had expected to back her, having him down firmly in the Samuelson camp. Clearly she had misjudged him. He seemed really excited as he went on, running his finger along a line of one of the xeroxes, commenting on the nervous intensity of the *p*s and *f*s, the hasty cross-over loops of the *g*s and *j*s which did not suggest the copyist. All of which made Samuelson madder. He barely glanced at the xeroxes, stood up, tugging at his beard, and made a pompous little speech saying it was well known – or at last it used to be well known, when people still read poetry, not just tedious feminist tracts – that Madoc, when inspired by some opiate, would often experience what he called the 'enthusiastic fit'. On such occasions, words and images would spew forth from him in an impassioned jumble, just like, as he once declared, the apostles at Pentecost, speaking in tongues. To those unskilled in deciphering his words, the things that Madoc uttered at such times might appear as hopeless nonsensical rant. Heaven help the poor copyist who attempted to create some sort of coherence from it. Only Jane could possibly have done so – only she could have managed to piece together the fugitive, trance-like creatures of his imagination, catching images on the wing like wild birds of paradise, and setting them in ink. *If* these manuscripts were genuine – which he very much doubted – but *if* they were, they *might* offer an illustration of that process at work. So that if they were genuine, they might be of genuine critical significance. But only if they could be rescued from the kind of mindless, modish feminist jargon to which they had just been subjected.

Morris was caught in something of a quandary. Ever since the rumour of the Oxford Chair had started, his manner had been one of scholarly correctness. For him the priority was to maintain the appropriate balance of scholarly enthusiasm and caution.

He would be fascinated to see the rest of the evidence – he said – though, from a cursory inspection and with the greatest respect to Professor Samuelson, the manuscripts did not appear to him in any way random, anarchic or the results of a drug-induced fantasy. People who thought like that, he ventured to suggest, were perhaps victims of their own psychedelic fantasies.

'Hear, hear,' said Carstairs.

It was generally agreed that further discussion of the manuscripts might be fruitfully postponed till the final Plenary Session, by which time everyone should have had an opportunity to consider the xeroxes and, with luck, the preliminary analysis from Bristol might be through. Outside the Hall, Danny caught up with Terry sitting on a bench and, most unusually for her, smoking.

'Congratulations,' he said, 'you're having quite a week.' She smiled.

'How d'you think it went?'

'Need to ask?'

'Still unconvinced?'

'Let's say, I reserve judgement.'

'Spoken like a true critic.'

'For your sake.'

'Oh no, not for my sake. I'm not the one that matters...' She smiled. 'Thanks, anyway.'

'For what?'

'Not standing up and opposing me.'

'What? And side with Samuelbum?' he laughed. 'Besides, I've got a vested interest.'

She squashed out her cigarette with her foot in the gravel. 'That was only if we didn't find anything,' she said.

'Was it?'

They looked at each other, then Danny stood up to go.

'Don't forget about tonight,' she said.

'I'll be there. Don't worry.'

8

As Danny walked back across the garden, a face smiled up at him, beside the rhododendrons. It was a face at the same time familiar and strange; the uncertain smile disturbed him with a feeling akin to guilt.

'I thought it was you.'

The face was fringed with hair, a beard, side-whiskers, moustache – all unkempt like a bad attempt at a disguise; the voice too, though unrecognisable, was dimly reminiscent, its dull grating monotone raised goose bumps all down his back. The body to which this hirsute face belonged coiled above him, tall and thin as a convolvulus.

'Nevill,' he said, turning the name into an apology. 'Of course.' The horror of recognition was instantaneous, bringing with it a nasal spasm, more a hiccup than a word, and a shrug as it all came flooding back. Like a bad conscience. Nevill wore green canvas gardening gloves several sizes too large for him: stained and cracked with earth and thorns, they made him appear oddly beast-like. In one hand he held a crushed bloom, in the other a secateurs. When Danny stuck out his hand to shake, Nevill became instantly nervous; he dropped the flower in the mud and struggled to tug his right glove off with his left.

'Sorry.'

He was one of the gardeners here; had been for over a year. They were very kind to him, he said, the Brethren. The place was nice and the pace of life was very soothing. After what he'd been through – he stopped, unable to continue, staring at the secateurs in his hand. He seemed oddly to belong to the garden, more like a scarecrow or a garden gnome than a human being. Quite suddenly, he began pruning rose-hips again, and the power of speech returned. Nevill said he had found Jesus and, for the first time in his life, was happy. He didn't *sound* very happy, Danny noticed; he didn't sound any happier than he'd done down the Cowley Road when he sat whingeing on about how he should have gone to Manchester. But here at the community he felt he belonged, he said. It was odd the way he only seemed able to talk while simultaneously pruning roses or plucking away convolvulus, as though talking could only be under-taken as a side effect from something else. The more he tore at overhanging foliage, the more voluble he became. Of course he wasn't a Brother – not yet – probably never would be – not a proper Brother. It was a very strict order, and the induction process took years. With his infallible instinct for self-mortification, Nevill was already a martyr to his chosen faith. Broken blooms, crimson and white, lay round his plimsolled feet. He tugged hard at a fallen tree, and words seemed to stick in his throat. There were things he wanted to say, but the words for them just wouldn't come. He tugged and tugged at the branches of an elm that had fallen in the storm which, two weeks previously, had cut off all the electricity.

'Can I help?'

Together they managed to ease the branches back from the bed of peonies and dahlias onto which they'd fallen and edge them towards the slope where George Madoc's original sylvan glade, now just a patch of brambles, had begun.

'Your hands!' said Nevill when they rested. Danny looked, and his hands were cut and bleeding. Nevill looked crestfallen. 'You hadn't any gloves.'

'Just scratches,' said Danny, caught between sounding natural and sounding like John Wayne. Something about the state of Danny's hands gave Nevill the urge to speak, and he blustered it out awkwardly, staring down at Danny's hands. He had forgiven him, he said. Jesus had given him the courage to forgive. Danny was mystified. Forgive him? For what? All that time at Oxford, Nevill replied, he had known that Danny was just like the rest of them – though, at the time, he pretended not to know. He thought it was something wrong with him – some kind of intelligence that he didn't have, a wavelength that he couldn't tune into. Danny was his friend; Danny had pretended to be on the same wavelength as him. But really he hadn't been; he could say that now. He knew that really Danny had been on a different wavelength all the time. Danny didn't know what to say. He felt expected to apologise but he wasn't sure what for. For putting up with Nevill's endless complaints? For being cleverer than Nevill?

Nevill led him through the lower parts of the garden, along the serpentine path that George Madoc had cunningly designed amid carefully chosen foliage, and down to the central clearing and the spring which George Madoc had ornamented with marble and dedicated to Apollo. The well still worked, and Nevill let down the bucket to draw up water to wash Danny's hands. This was very kind of him, of course; but there was something uncomfortably reverential, even ritualistic about the business, that made Danny's flesh creep. Nevill insisted on bathing Danny's hands himself, carefully washing away all trace of blood and massaging each finger with a touch strangely soft for a gardener, soft like a woman. All the time he washed he talked, not looking up, not looking Danny in the face, but staring at their hands there intertwined, Danny's and his own. For a long while after Oxford – he was saying – he felt anger in his heart for Danny, real anger for the way that he behaved. The blades of Nevill's secateurs gleamed in the thigh pocket of his dungarees and, for a moment, Danny had the horrifying thought that Nevill was going to snap off one of his fingers like the twigs that he was tending. But Jesus had saved him. Jesus had rescued him from his anger. Jesus had granted him the victory over himself. The hands were now perfectly clean, and Nevill held his clasped together before his face in a prayerful gesture. With a gaze full of solemn unction he proclaimed: 'I forgive you'. It was like a heavy weight falling upon Danny's shoulders. Being forgiven was the most incriminating experience he could remember. He felt an overwhelming desire to smash

Nevill full in the face, but no doubt Nevill would have forgiven him for that as well. He might even have glorified in it. It would have given him another opportunity to gain the victory over himself – as a holy martyr.

They walked back towards the Hurst: Nevill cheerful, Danny furious and silent. Something else he ought to know – said Nevill. He knew that awful man McWhinnie was here too. He'd seen him in town buying sausages.

'Sausages?'

'Pork chippolatas. Yesterday, in Kennedy's. 'Course he never recognised me. People never do.'

Danny wasn't listening anymore. He was trying to make sense of the fact that McWhinnie was here, but not here. In town, but not at the conference? What was he playing at? The point was, said Nevill, that he really couldn't find it in his heart to forgive him. Not McWhinnie. He knew it was wrong. He knew it was a sin. He knew he should be able to forgive him – but he couldn't. He'd tried. He'd prayed and prayed, but it was no use. He stopped and looked Danny full in the face.

'I'm sorry,' he said, 'but I still hate that man.'

Carstairs and Powell-Davies sat gazing down the porch of Glendower Hall. Down the slope, the neat ornamental lawn, bordered with marigolds and pansies, curved away either side of the gravelled drive. It was dusk, and the last crimson rays of the sun bathed the worn stonework of the statue of Hippocrates with a soft roseate glow. Still there was a sharp wind as usual, over Plynlimon Fawr, and Powell-Davies had a tartan rug – a plaid, she called it – wrapped about her knees. Deceptively damp, the evening mists, she warned. All too easy to take a chill – and she offered Carstairs a corner of her rug. Carstairs didn't really think of himself as the kind of chap who needed to sit with a tartan rug over his knees. All the same, there was a certain dampness in the air, and there was something undoubtedly congenial about sitting here, staring at the sunset, sharing a tartan rug with this game old bird as she rambled on about her time in India. So he accepted her offer and beamed as she pulled her chair closer and set about tucking the plaid snugly round both their knees. She started telling him the history of the plaid, from her mother's uncle's family in Manitoba, which accounted for the slightly discrepant pattern, because it was recalled from memory alone. Carstairs passed her the flask, and they both took a nip of neat gin which burnt their throats, flushed their cheeks and made them feel ever so mellow. Their fingers touched as she handed back the flask. Carstairs thought it a very agreeable plaid, a handsome tartan with the slight variation to its patterning all to the good. If one examined similar slight transformations of even the most traditional designs – insignia, flags and coats-of-arms – one discovered the same processes at work. Sometimes there was a temptation to simplify, at other times, to embellish; in that way the basic design was constantly renewed, uniting tradition with individual skill. Powell-Davies beamed at him – her face, in the golden twilight seeming much younger, almost schoolgirl-like in its enthusiasm. It wasn't often she spent an evening like this, listening and talking to a man with such evident intelligence and good taste. She couldn't resist telling him so – and Carstairs gave her an extra nip of gin. Just then he thought he felt something, a nudge of some kind, her knee against his, under the plaid; only he couldn't be sure. That kind of thing could easily happen quite by accident under a plaid but, all the same, Carstairs was feeling pretty good by now, and he nudged back. Powell-Davies' knee didn't move, but allowed itself to be rubbed gently, up and down, while Carstairs experienced the delicious tingle of worsted against tweed. Saturday would be his big day, she said, not looking at him, face turned to the sunset, allowing her knee to be rubbed up and down – the toast to the immortal memory, beside the fatal pool. Carstairs sighed and said that he didn't mind telling her, in confidence, he'd be glad when the whole affair was over. Since McWhinnie had gone AWOL, things had just got out of hand. She was sure he would cope, she said; he seemed the kind of man who could cope with most things. Carstairs thought to himself, with a certain self-satisfaction, that he could still work the charm; even now he still had what it took. Fancy, a tough old bird like this one, and now look at her. He did look at her, and she at him; he held her hand – or maybe she held his, difficult to say who began it – but it seemed just the most natural thing in the world to do. Similarly, just a few seconds later, both felt exceedingly silly to be sitting there holding hands in the sunlight, and, as a descant to that thought there came, from the far side of the B4521, the sound of someone, male, singing. At first the sounds of song were wafted fitfully, in the wind, and it seemed quite enchanting: a lonely serenade. Carstairs felt Powell-Davies give his fingers a slight squeeze. As the voice drew nearer, there seemed something slightly raucous about the intonation: the tune was something recognisable from the chapel hymnal, though Carstairs could not name it. But, though the singing was entirely in Welsh, it seemed probable – if only from the crudeness of the intonation – that the words were not authentic. This suspicion hardened when, on the utterance of two short syllables, he felt Powell-Davies' fingers stiffen before she withdrew her hand. The singer was now in view: half-silhouetted in the twilight, he stood at the bottom of the lawn, leaning unsteadily on a statue of Virtue. He staggered a little, stopped singing, and there was a long ominous silence; then he raised his head and shoulders, as though pumping himself up, stood erect and began to wail, at the top of his voice: '*Mad-oc*! *Mad-oc*!'

The figure then bent down, gathered up pebbles and stones and hurled them in the direction of the Hall. His aim was hopeless, and most fell harmlessly on the lawn, though one or two came close to the windows. Lights went on in the Parry Madoc building and faces appeared at the windows, looking out. Maybe they should retire to a safer vantage-point, Carstairs suggested, but Powell-Davies insisted on staying right where she was. 'Nonsense,' she said, 'it's only Gwilliam on one of his binges.'

'You know that man?' said Carstairs.

She turned on him a mischievous smile he found rather disturbing.

'I should,' she said. 'I used to be married to him.'

They met behind the summer-house a little after eleven. Terry's skilful engineering of each separate element in the revenge plot revealed a flair for stratagems which Danny, who considered himself a connoisseur of such manoeuvres, viewed with admiration. It was her patient attention to detail which demonstrated her finesse. For example the spotlight, high up under the eaves of the summer-house, normally shone across the pool at night; but Terry had located the master switch and turned it off. Usually, too, the little wicket-gate across the pathway from the shrubbery to the southside of the pool was locked at dusk; but somehow Terry had procured a key. Even her planning of his own role in the escapade, though unflattering to his dignity, reinforced his admiration for her style. He was, at her insistence, got up in one of the Brethren's brown serge cassocks, stolen from the Dean's laundry room.

'I can't bloody move in this,' he said on first trying it on. The thing dragged around his ankles.

'That's fine,' she said. 'That's how they wear them. Don't forget the hood.'

In the darkness, heavy pleats kept catching on thorns as, having met Babs by the wicket-gate, the three of them crept down to the pool by torchlight and hid among the bushes.

'I suppose he will fall for all this,' he said, tugging himself free from thickets on his left side only to be caught in brambles on his right. 'I mean, it is *him* you're trying to get?'

Terry grinned. 'Oh yes,' she said. 'Who else?'

It was possible to detect Samuelson's approach from some distance, as he stumbled and crashed through the shrubbery without the benefit of a torch, missing his footing, colliding with tree stumps and lurching into shrubs. He was panting heavily, and the night air carried some strange aroma from him. It was something he put on his beard, an expensive toiletry with an oddly industrial smell, like kitchen cleanser, which clashed violently with the delicate fragrance of the night-scented stocks. Suddenly there was a low groan as he crashed into something in the darkness. Terry prodded Babs.

'Now,' she whispered.

Babs – her face cold and hard – nevertheless assumed a sultry, siren voice. 'Over here,' she called out; then she paused and added, with a quite malicious intimacy: 'Larry.'

'What? Where are you?' he called out with a kind of desperate urgency, trying to sound romantic, yet having obvious difficulty in entirely suppressing a note of irritation. 'I can't see a bloody thing!'

As if in confirmation, there was the sound of another painful collision. Babs called out to him again, 'Over here!' and took a couple of steps forward as Terry and Danny kept back behind a rhododendron. Now at last Samuelson's outline became visible, a faint pale shape against the blackness of the trees, panting like a steam engine.

'Oh, there you are,' he whispered, clearly relieved to make out her approaching presence. 'I...'

Without giving him a moment to regain his breath, Babs launched herself at him, held him tight and glued his mouth with a kiss. Samuelson was overwhelmed, flailing with his arms. Then, just as suddenly, she let go.

'Take your clothes off,' she breathed into his ear.

'Wait,' he tried to steady himself, leaning against a tree.

'No, now!' she commanded. Her hands went straight for his trouser-belt, yanking at the fastening.

'Just give me a minute!' He tried to back away, struggling with his jacket, but she wouldn't let him.

'Come on, all of them.' She tugged at his fly-zip and his trousers crumpled to the ground. Poor Samuelson, it was pathetic to watch the astonished, desperate eagerness with which his fingers fumbled and tore at the rest of his clothes. At last he stood before her, stark naked except for his socks. He stretched out his hands towards her.

'And those,' she whispered, pointing to his socks.

'Oh really, I don't think…' he began, but she shook her head.

'It's more fun this way,' assuming a lasciviously determined voice she bent forward and brushed her lips over his chest hair. 'I promise.' All this while Babs was careful to remove as few of her own clothes as possible. She began with an elaborate display of shedding a clinging white sweater, and now, to keep him keen, went into a striptease routine with her stockings. But she was safely covered up, where it mattered most, with wired bra and two thick pairs of knickers. When he'd pulled off his socks she took him by the hand and drew him nearer to the pool.

'Over here. I know the perfect spot.'

'Come on, Babs, wherever… Ouch!' Samuelson's bare feet were tender on the broken, pebble-strewn ground. He was getting very excited.

'Trust me, Larry, you'll love it.' She led him to the pre-arranged place, carefully marked out by herself and Terry earlier in the day with a line of four small bright white pebbles. She knelt down, just to the left of the pebbles.

'Here,' she said, pulling him towards her. 'Can't you smell the honeysuckle?'

Samuelson, stark naked, eagerly lowered himself down beside her. There was a pause, a long moment as anticipated rapture turned to disbelief. Then he started yelling.

'Jesus! What is this? I'm burning!' Desperately scrabbling in the ground behind him, he drew up a fistful of foliage.

'Bloody nettles!'

She had led him directly to the nettle-patch. Babs leapt up, without a word.

'You bitch! You bloody little bitch! Just you wait...' he yelled, trying to grab hold of her. That was Terry and Danny's cue. Rushing forward in their robed disguise, hoods plucked down to hide their faces, they suddenly seized hold of Samuelson, hoisted him each by an arm, carried him bodily forward, still yelling, to the side of the pool, and threw him over the edge. He made a terrific splash as he hit the water.

'Still burning, Larry?' shouted Babs, suddenly sounding adult and rather sharp. 'That should cool you off.'

'Quickly, the clothes, the clothes...' whispered Terry. They bundled Samuelson's things into a black bin liner she'd brought along.

'You bitch! Get me out. I'm drowning!... I'm drowning!...' wailed Samuelson.

'Got everything?' said Terry, making for the wicket-gate.

'Help! Heelp! I can't swim! I'm drowning!...' Samuelson's cries were increasingly desperate.

'Think he's all right?' asked Danny, and Terry paused, listening for a moment.

'Yeah,' she nodded. 'Bluff, pure bluff...'

As a final touch, after locking the wicket-gate behind them, Terry switched on the pool spotlight. There, in the middle of the pool, the white mound of Samuelson's belly floated on the surface like ghostly blanc-mange.

'Help! Heelp! I'm drowning!...'

Terry's idea was to chuck the bin liner with all Samuelson's clothes in it over the wall of the garden into the female Brothers quarters.

'Just let him try explaining that.'

As the three of them hurried down the path, they saw another robed figure scurrying towards them. Evidently one of the female Brothers who had been alerted by Samuelson's cries of distress. They watched as Brother Edith unlocked the wicket-gate and ran down towards the pool.

'Help! Help!' cried Samuelson.

Brother Edith peeled off her heavy robe to reveal thick wollen combination underwear – as prescribed – which fully covered her arms and legs. She was about to dive in when, as Samuelson flopped over in the water, belly sinking and buttocks rising, she became aware of his nakedness.

'You've got no clothes on!' she cried out, horrified.

'I'm drowning!...' Samuelson's voice was becoming weak as he swallowed yet another mouthful of water.

'I can't come in there. Not with you naked like that.'

'Heelp! For God's sake, get me out!...' This time he submerged completely for several seconds, till his head bobbed up again, spluttering and choking. 'Heeeelp!'

For Brother Edith this was a serious moral dilemma. She considered throwing him her own discarded robe but knew that, waterlogged, it would only drag him down.

'Please,' he wailed.

At last she made a decision.

'I will close my eyes,' she announced. 'You keep on calling out. I'll follow the sound of your voice. Do try and keep your back turned to me though, just in case.'

With that, she dove into the water and began paddling, backwards, towards him.

'Help!... Oh, help... help... help...' he moaned, his voice sinking like a clockwork toy whose motor was running down. She reached him and, taking him by the shoulders, drew him towards the steps.

'Just you wait there,' she insisted, clambering out of the water, 'till I get something to cover you up.' She ran to the place where she'd left her robe and was astonished to find it had gone. Behind the hedge Terry was hugging herself with delight. No matter how well you planned these things, some of the best touches are sheer chance.

'I don't believe it... where is it?' Brother Edith hunted up and down. 'It can't just have vanished!'

But it had. There was no sign of it anywhere. Meanwhile Samuelson was beginning to haul himself, painfully, out of the pool. Strangely, to judge by appearances, the evening's misadventures and the coolness of the water had had little effect on his ardour – rather the contrary, in fact.

'You can't come out yet,' she cried. 'Not like *that*.'
But Samuelson was already out.

'Where can it be? Where can it be?' Brother Edith sounded increasingly distraught, desperately looking everywhere but at him.

'My clothes have disappeared too,' he said.

'But how?'

Samuelson shrugged. As Terry had anticipated, the whole thing was too hugely embarrassing for him to attempt any kind of explanation.

'I'm very grateful to you,' he said, stumbling towards her.

'Don't come any closer.'

'I might have drowned.'

'You stay where you are.'

'Please,' he reached out his hand towards her.

'Don't touch me!'

'I only wanted to say...' His outstretched hand glanced her elbow. Brother Edith sprang away as if touched by an electric cable.

'Leave me alone!' she yelled, clenching her two fists together, then swinging them hard and catching him a full hard blow on the side of the face. 'You animal!' She ran off into the bushes.

'Shit.' Samuelson, toppling backwards from the blow, put his hand out to save himself, but it was no use. He fell back into the nettle-patch.

'Shit! Shit! Shit!' he yelled.

In the darkness the conspirators exulted. Such a comprehensive triumph was beyond even Terry's dreams. Babs walked back quite happily to her room in the Hall.

'Congratulations,' said Danny, catching Terry's hand. 'Now, about my reward...'

'I haven't forgotten,' she said, pushing him away, 'but we have unfinished business.'

She gave him an antiseptic kiss and looked away, her face suddenly serious. She needed separation between them; intimacy might betray her into feelings she couldn't control.

'Tomorrow,' she said, suddenly.

'Why not now?'

She shook her head rather quickly; for the first time he sensed a certain indecision in her reaction, which only made him want her more. He sensed she was not arguing with him but with herself.

'Don't forget to put back your robe,' she called out, without turning. Already she was planning, contriving, scheming once more. The moment had passed. He watched her figure grow pale as she walked back among the trees.

9

'Sausages?'

'Chippolatas.'

Morris placed his arms very deliberately on the arms of the chair, closed his eyes, elongated his neck and took several deep breaths. He was trying, very hard, to see the funny side, he said. He assumed there *was* a funny side? Danny shrugged. Morris supposed *someone* should go into town and look for him.

'Don't look at me.'

'I can't go. I'm chairman…'

'Ask Samuelson. He's got his Capri.'

'Oh *no*. Look, normally I wouldn't ask…'

'And normally I'd go.'

'But?'

'No transport.'

Morris thought for a while, sighed, pulled out his car keys and chucked them across the table.

'Just don't have a crash, that's all. I don't think I could take that.'

Hancock was always game for a tour of the local pubs. He thought the 'sausages' quip, when he heard it, was a touch of sheer genius.

'You've got to hand it to the old bugger –' he said.

Morris had given Danny various bits of cautionary advice about the car. Third gear was a bit sticky, and the rear tyres were rather worn; so best go easy on the bends and stick to under fifty.

'Bomb it along,' said Hancock, once they were out the gates. 'Let's see what it'll do.'

He yanked off a little 'No Smoking' sign that dangled from the driver's mirror, chucked it out the window and proceeded to declaim the entire *Declaration des Droits de l'Homme* in a sonorous French accent, sitting in the front seat, knees hunched, feet resting on the dashboard. In town, a winding traffic jam stretched back from the first lights they came to. Hancock was delighted. 'Market-day,' he announced. 'Boozers'll be open all day.' A gaunt youth with a beard and a blonde girl in singlet and jeans worked slowly down the row of cars, handing out leaflets in Welsh. Some English rhetoric at the foot of the page announced that the usurpers would be driven from the land by fire and sword, and the children of freedom would sing from the hills to the shore. This was apparently an allusion to a prophecy of Merlin contained in the *Mabinogion*, though unfamiliar to both Danny and Hancock.

'Nats,' said Hancock, screwing the thing up and chucking it out the window.

In town there were Nats everywhere. Outside Woolworths, in the market square, a youth in dark glasses spouted Welsh through a loud-hailer mounted on the back of a pick-up van which was painted all over in red-and-green Nat slogans. A girl, green ribbons in her hair, hung from the front window, eating a hot dog and leering at the passers-by. The youth's amplified words, delivered in an upbeat monotone, so rapid and indistinct as to be unintelligible even by Welsh speakers, echoed round the colonnades, or were lost in revving engines, barking dogs and crying kids. Every so often the youth would stop, and the van would play snatches of *Men of Harlech* on a scratchy record, to which the kids gathered round the ice-cream stall all knew different versions. There were Nats all round the square, in the alleys leading to the bus station and the Highfields shopping complex, with leaflets, badges, petitions, banners and collection boxes. In the warm sun, with brightly coloured shirts and banners, they gave the old town a festival air. Leaving the car in the multi-storey, they made for the Old Red Lion and, as Hancock had predicted, it was full of elderly red-faced gents in pork-pie hats and rough tweeds smelling strongly of dung and pipe-tobacco. A pair of collies sprawled across most of the floor. The barman had never heard of McWhinnie, but there had been a queer sort of Englishman, one of your stuck-up types, reading his *Daily Telegraph* in the bar last night, complaining it had taken him all day to lay his hands on a copy. Not much call for the *Daily Telegraph* in these parts. 'Sure, but I read it.'

A roly-poly figure leant forward from behind them and grinned. His wrinkled face was entirely circled with white hair, like some kind of tropical flower; his mildewed corduroys stretched tight across his tubby thighs like beer barrels, and the waistband of his trousers was pulled halfway up his chest. He wore a greasy hounds-tooth jacket with a paisley scarf spewing out of the top pocket, down to his lap.

'This McWhinnie fella,' he said in a kind of drawl, elbowing himself forward and grinning, 'that wouldn't by any chance be McWhinnie R.F., the editor of Madoc?'

There was something ominous about the way he said it, pronouncing each word with a thick Welsh accent which, though no doubt perfectly accurate, sounded just like Peter Sellers. The word 'editor', in particular, echoed like a metropolitan sexual perversity, and for just a moment Danny thought that this might *be* McWhinnie. It was exactly the kind of Sherlock Holmes effect that might appeal to him.

'Gwilliam ap Gwyndwr,' the man said sonorously, leaving them baffled. 'You are not, I see, familiar with my works.' He raised both eyebrows, first one and then the other, rocking himself from side to side and flapping his paisley scarf like a pennant.

'Ap?' said Hancock, hopefully.

'Gwyndwr,' he repeated, elongating the syllables to create a phonetic boomerang effect. He cleared his throat and began to recite something in Welsh. His voice rose and bubbled like water cascading in a flood; dribbles of spit hung from his lips, and his face went purple with the effort. It was odd how his tubby body, so cramped and squashed, became animated as soon as he began to orate. It was like some Heath-Robinson bagpipe, forcing air up from his beer-barrel thighs, through the stumpy bellows of his middle. The words were sung, not spoken, a continuous keening cry, not at all beautiful – rather ugly in fact in its heavy, breathy insistence, but moving nevertheless. It filled the pub with its serious sound, rising and falling like an angry wind, and someone turned off the TV racing at Chepstow. He seemed unconcerned by all the attention, sitting there, eyes closed, face red, filling the air with his song. It was easy to tell when he had reached the last stanza: the tempo slowed, and each syllable was drawn out in a melancholy drone. A man at the bar, tartan cap on his head and white poodle under his arm, had tears in his eyes. Gwilliam's own eyes were streaming as he strained to a final crescendo, raising his voice upwards to the ceiling. When it was done, there was a tremendous roar of applause. Gwilliam took the scarf from his pocket and wiped his face.

'And what would McWhinnie R.F. make of that?' he demanded. No doubt he'd want to see it all written down. Well, it wasn't written down, and it never *would be* written down. Kills it, that does. He must have recited that poem a hundred times. At least – he said. And every time it was different. Every time. No two times ever the same. He looked from the one to the other of them, with the same cocky grin on his face. 'If once you tried to write it all down,' he said, 'you would kill it. Kill it stone dead. All you would have would be a dead thing, a corpse, ready for nothing but studying in a university.'

Hancock went to the bar, while Danny tried to find out more about McWhinnie. Gwilliam had great fun teasing him. How you could hope to teach people poetry was what he would never understand, he said. He'd said as much to their man, the great McWhinnie R.F. himself from Oxford University. 'Sitting right there, he was – right where you are now. I said to him, you try to teach me the meaning of a Madoc poem and I'll knock you down flat. And I would have, too. You don't teach poetry – you feel it. It isn't in the brain, but in the blood!' He slapped the table, hard.

'It's in the beer, more like,' said a fellow at the bar, and Gwilliam grinned. 'That too,' he said, belching vigorously.

On the subject of McWhinnie he was adamant: the man was a charlatan and a fraud. Madoc was a creation of the English tourist industry. They should cease studying the works of Madoc immediately. They should erase Madoc's name from the syllabus. He had told McWhinnie this. Why? Why, that was obvious. Madoc had stolen the guts of his poems – the ones that had any guts – from the Celtic bards. All Madoc had done was tart them up to appeal to the English ladies. Add to this the fact that the man was a liar, a pervert, a traitor and very probably a murderer too…

It was impossible to tell how much of all this was an act, and Gwilliam professed total ignorance – and unconcern – about McWhinnie's whereabouts now. Hancock kept feeding him whiskies, and every so often Gwilliam would break into another droning Celtic incantation, muttering over the brim on his glass, before lapsing back to silence. Maybe he knew something and maybe he didn't – either way, he wasn't saying…

They got back late that afternoon, and Danny reported his findings to Morris.

'He's here all right,' he said, reporting *almost* what Gwyndwr had said. 'But *where*, exactly?…' Morris sat down heavily. This was all he needed, he said. If McWhinnie were here, and coming to give the Memorial Lecture, then that was fine. That would be *almost* as the programme indicated. Failing that, if he were *not* here, then it was no doubt a pity and so on, but Morris had been doing some serious thinking, and he believed he could cope with that. A great deal of shifting would be necessary, and it all really depended on whether Professor Franks got word from Bristol. But this! Morris sighed, audibly. As if this weren't enough, all morning he'd had complaints from the Brethren about Samuelson.

'Samuelson?'

'Apparently he's been swimming in the pool without a costume. Which is bad enough. But then, to cap it all, last night he propositioned Brother Edith! She's written to Seattle all about it. I had the Dean himself in here half an hour ago demanding that Samuelson makes her a personal face-to-face apology. And *confesses* (his word) exactly what he intended.

Otherwise he threatens to cancel the rest of the programme. Which, as things are going, might be no bad thing. I tell you I am never *ever* doing anything like this again.'

Danny went up to Block B and knocked on Terry's door.

'Who is it?' she snapped in a voice which could not be considered welcoming. Danny said who it was.

'What do you want?' said Terry, maintaining her aggressive tone. 'Look, I'm busy.'

'Well, first I'd like to be let in.'

There was a lengthy wait, and then at last Terry came to the door and opened it a couple of inches.

'Well? What is it? Because whatever it is, there is nothing I can do about it.'

'Is there someone with you?' asked Danny, puzzled by her tone. She became immediately defensive.

'No. Of course not. Why ever do you ask?'

'You seem on edge, that's all.'

Terry relaxed a fraction, even put on a smile. 'OK,' she said. 'Only I've got masses to do. You can come in, but literally only for five minutes.' She threw open the door and, rather ostentatiously, looked at her watch. This was her big chance, she said. She'd been on the phone to her friend Rory in New York, who was terribly excited, and phoned someone she knew at one of the leading agencies. And what do you know? She had only just been talking to Shirley Weissmann from Shrew!

'Shrew?'

'Shrew. You must know them. They're only the biggest feminist publishing house in the States.'

'Congratulations,' he said, coldly.

'Yeah, but now I have to handle it very carefully.' Terry began to pace the meagre floor space of the room. 'I've got them all here.'

'Them?' said Danny, innocently.

'You know what I mean. Everyone alive who's ever worked on Madoc.'

'Except McWhinnie,' he said, and she smiled. 'OK, apart from McWhinnie. So if I'm going to make a stand on Jane Madoc, this is the place to do it. It all depends on Bristol. I've been onto Watters in the micro-what's-it lab. He says they can probably let me have a preliminary report by tomorrow evening. I'm paying him to get it to me first thing. Assuming McWhinnie doesn't show up, I'll have an hour to convince them – or some of them – about Jane Madoc. Mid-Wales radio say they may send someone down, and the Merthyr Chronicle are definitely coming, but Shirley says just to give them a taster. Of course, I don't expect to get an easy ride. Samuelson's beyond hope. But maybe he won't turn up. Speaking of which, what have you heard?'

'How long have I got,' said Danny, looking at his watch. For the first time a genuine smile spread across Terry's face. 'Oh, all right, I know what you're thinking. But this is important. To me, at least. When I came here, to this conference, I hadn't the faintest idea who either of the Madocs were. Which may be an advantage, I don't know. But since I found the manuscripts...'

'Since *we* found the manuscripts.'

Terry stopped. 'Sorry,' she said, and sounded genuinely contrite. 'God! I'll be glad when this is over. I wasn't meaning to belittle your role. Actually, I think it strengthens our claim. The discovery was partly made by a man. Shirley wasn't too keen on including you in the contract, but I insisted. This way, when they start complaining that... what's up? Where are you going?'

'Don't worry. My mistake. I thought you'd be in a more receptive frame of mind.'

'Receptive? *Oh*, you mean...' She blushed. She'd forgotten all about the wager – which, he supposed, was quite charming. In its way.

'I hope it all goes well,' he said, opening the door.

'Wait.' She rushed over and closed it again. 'I haven't forgotten.' She spoke low, her tone completely changed.

'You give a good impression of it.'

'I just need time.'

'Of course.'

'Don't be like that.'

'How should I be?'

They stared at each other for a couple of seconds until he saw her black eyes lowered. He opened the door. 'See you at the Plenary Session,' he began, but she stopped him.

'What's the time?' she asked.

'Six minutes later than when I came in,' he said, 'for which I profoundly apologise.'

She took a deep breath, drew herself up and, narrowing her eyes, looked at him. 'All right,' she said. 'Midnight. I shall come to you tonight at midnight. You know it's midsummer's night?'

'I wasn't going to say. I trust the ass's head is optional?'

'As you please.'

'You'll come to my room?'

'No.'

'Where then?'

'Can't you guess?'

He looked into her black eyes and saw dark passions tingling.

As Danny made his way along the central corridor, around eleven-thirty, he heard a loud crash in the Llewellyn lounge, followed by sounds of a man's voice, whimpering. Danny pushed open the door and looked round to see Samuelson, sprawled out across a sofa, moaning. Beside him several chairs, a coffee table and a lamp lay upturned on the floor. Danny approached him, warily.

'Hullo.'

Samuelson only wore one shoe; the other lay squashed beneath the coffee table.

'Are you all right?'

'All right?' Samuelson raised his head an inch or

two, blinked and stared. 'Am I all *right*?' he said, then sank back again, moaning.

'Here.'

Trying to help him sit up, Danny took hold of a shoulder and promptly ducked when Samuelson took a swing at him. Danny noticed a whisky bottle cradled against his thigh.

'Leave me alone,' he growled.

'My pleasure,' he started to walk away.

'No, no. Don't *go*.' Samuelson rolled his eyes, pathetically.

'Make up your mind.'

Eventually, with assistance, Samuelson managed to sit up and stared gloomily at Danny.

'You know how it is,' he said, 'it's not the brainy ones who get you. They never drive you mad. It's the stupid ones. The brainy ones are all too keen to be part of your world; they want to be just like you. What's attractive about that? That's not attractive – it's repulsive. It's grotesque. I always run a mile from the brainy ones. But the stupid ones!' He groaned, poured himself another scotch and took a photo from his top pocket. It was fuzzy, indistinct, of a girl with blonde hair.

'She was the stupidest of the lot. Proud of it. Boasted about it. In three whole years she never read a single book. Not one. Even now that takes some doing on an Eng. Lit. course. She got a degree – a third – just what she wanted. Anything more, she said, would be an insult to the system. She said to me,

the night after her last exam, don't you go fixing
nothing. She knew maybe I could raise her up a notch
or two – don't you lay a finger on those marks. Those
are *my* marks and I don't want anybody touching
them. She was lying on my bed, I remember; it was
the first time she was there on my bed. She said…' –
he paused and looked up – 'you don't mind if I say
this? Oh, to hell with it, I don't care if you mind or
not…' – he slurped another scotch – 'she took my
finger, this finger here, and…' – he stopped suddenly,
drew a deep breath, and there were tears cascading
down his cheeks. 'I'm sorry,' he said.

Danny said there wasn't any reason to feel embarrassed, but Samuelson heard it the other way round;
when Danny added, for good measure, that he wasn't
in the least embarrassed, Samuelson took it as a jibe.

'Oh,' he said, feeling instantly enraged with him.
'Good for you!'

Sensing the changed tone, Danny stood up to go,
but Samuelson beckoned him to stay.

'Don't go,' he said pathetically, his anger subsiding
as quickly as it began. He started talking about his first
wife, who never had a degree. Left school at fifteen
and went to work in a shop. With her it was always
the words she loved. Words fascinated her. He used to
read to her, from a dictionary, night after night.

'We did crossword puzzles in bed. No, please don't
go,' Samuelson said, seeing the desire to leave in
Danny's eyes. He turned out his pockets and, in
among loose change and paper tissues, he found some

brightly coloured letters children use to learn to read. He rearranged them on the table: they spelt out 'I LOVE YOU'.

'Old habits,' he said. The whisky bottle was empty. Danny didn't mind that Samuelson had hogged it all to himself. What he did mind though, now that it was empty, was Samuelson becoming very solicitous on his behalf. 'Poor sod,' he kept saying, 'you never got a drink,' turning the bottle upside down to make certain sure. 'Can't go on much longer,' he said, suddenly. 'Rationally, I do know that. And I accept it. Rationally I know it's over. It's just a matter of when.' He had the bottleneck grasped in his right hand and was swinging it with a thwack into his left. 'Every time I come away I wonder, is this it? Every time I think, this could be it.' Danny, playing thoughtlessly with the letters on the table, came up with 'O YOU VILE', and Samuelson stopped and looked at them as if transfixed.

'I never wanted to come here. I never do. I never want to leave her. I love her, everything about her. Everything. Do you know what that means?' He stared aggressively at Danny, poking his ribs with the bottle, 'do you? It's what everybody says, isn't it? "I love everything about you"; but they don't mean it. Not really. Most people, what they love is…' – he held up his hand and indicated a tiny gap between his finger and thumb – 'like that. But not me. I mean it. I love everything about that bitch. I love the way she gobbles her hamburgers and smears ketchup all over her hands. I love how she can't spell. I love the way she cuts her toe-nails in bed, the way she litters the house with coke cans and McDonald's boxes. People seem to think I can't see what she's done to me; they pity me. I see it, in their faces. They think I'm off my trolley...' – he paused and beckoned Danny nearer. 'Come here,' he said, 'let me talk to you. Come here.' He pulled his chair close, and Danny could feel the whisky breath in his face. 'I used to drive a Volvo. Most sensible car on the road. You couldn't get a more sensible car than that Volvo. But Lorna said it made her puke. I could either have her, or the Volvo, she said, but not both. So I got shot of the Volvo. The Capri was her idea – saw it in a breaker's yard. Even then, after I'd bought it, she wouldn't go the *whole hog* in it till I got those leopardskin seats. So, what d'you think of that, eh? What's your opinion of that?'

Danny thought it best to keep his opinion to himself.

'You think I'm mad? Well, I'll tell you what I am. I'm free! That's what I am, and it's what you'll never be. Free!' He raised himself, unsteadily, to his feet, and bellowed the word as loud as he was able: 'Free!...'

Over-balancing against the coffee table, he toppled over, came crashing to the floor and lay there, motionless, eyes closed, snoring. Lifting him by the shoulders, Danny dragged Samuelson across the floor, wedged him beside the sofa, untied his remaining shoe, and left.

The spotlight shining over the pool seemed somehow less bright than before, and the breeze rippling the waters was cold rather than invigorating. The sides of the pool were ghostly pale.

'Is this such a good idea?' said Danny as they both, side by side, looked down. Terry nodded. 'You first,' she said. Danny removed his jacket, tie and shoes, which scraped the gravel as he knelt to untie them. She stood and watched him. He felt completely unembarrassed by her gaze as she came forward, unbuttoned his shirt and ran her hands across his chest.

'Now,' she said when he was naked. Instantly he dived in and found the water cold, striking chill against his arms and legs. He felt a sudden panic of breathlessness as his stomach muscles contracted, and he stretched down to touch bottom, the water lapping at his chest.

'What's it like?'

'Cold,' he said, 'but wonderful.'

Letting go the edge, he struck out for the deep end, where darkness was total, and his teeth began to chatter. It was so cold the pleasure of the motion was almost indistinguishable from an agreeable numbness. He raised his hand, but was unable to see it in the darkness. It was as if his body had disappeared. He had no sense of individual arms, legs or feet; just of an enveloping sensation of exhilaration that didn't belong to his body, but was part of this dark universe. He couldn't tell if it were pain or pleasure he was experiencing; all sense of discrimination had vanished.

He couldn't tell where his body ended and the world of water began. Lying back, floating there, he could see the stars above him, but they seemed closer and more tangible than any earthly thing. This is what death must be like – he thought – one of those stars must be heaven.

'Danny,' Terry's voice crept over the stillness of the water like a mist. He raised his head to look for her. The spotlight marked out a silver pathway on the water – and beyond, he assumed, was Terry, naked and pale as a ghost. 'Are you OK?'

He slid back through the element, reaching the pool edge as she slipped her legs into the water. His outstretched arms touched and felt her body, more real to him now than his own. He touched her face, came close and kissed it. She wrapped her body close around his, and its warmth, in the coldness of the waters, was magical. From far off they heard the distant chime of the Hurst clock tolling midnight.

'This is wonderful. You…'

'Shh!' she said, and held him tight, kissing him again.

'BANG!'

There was the sound of a loud explosion, and Danny thought he caught a glimpse of something flashing in the darkness.

'What the hell was that?'

'I don't know. It sounded like…'

'BANG!' The second detonation sounded even closer. This time there was no mistaking the flash of a gun in the darkness, or the splash as something large fell in the water.

'Bloody hell! Terry! Terry! Are you all right?'

'Yes. What was it?'

'God knows. Bloody hell, I'm getting out.'

'Eh, wait for me! Come on, quickly. God! This water's cold. Is that your hand? Come on.'

Terry and Danny made their way to the far side of the pool, hauled their freezing bodies out and, without stopping to dry or properly dress themselves, hobbled back to the main part of the Hurst.

10

The water's character had completely altered over-night: no longer picture-postcard blue, it was cloudy, green opaque. Over the surface spread a scum of lar-vae and dead insects; down below algae smearing the bottom like a mould. The body was face upwards, its grey eyes open, dressed like a tailor's dummy in a dark suit with a gentle agitation wafting the college tie. A police diver in a wet suit lugged it to a corner, ready to be hoisted out.

'Did he have any enemies?'

Carstairs thought for a while. 'I might,' he said, 'ask you the same.'

The Inspector didn't follow.

'In the same line of business, you might say. McWhinnie was a literary critic. An upholder of the literary law. Passing judgements; chastising literary malefactors. A critic can't help making enemies. Recrimination's his natural habitat – it goes with the job. A better question might be, did he have any friends?'

'Well, did he?'

'Acquaintances, more like. Colleagues.' Carstairs didn't know of anybody close.

Danny explained about swimming in the pool the night before, and hearing the sounds of gunfire.

'You're sure that was what you heard?'

Danny said he hadn't much familiarity with gunfire. It might have been a car backfiring; but at the time he had had no doubt. The police did not stay long. They arranged to take statements from Terry, Danny and some others in the morning. Their attitude was very matter-of-fact; only when they had gone did the real detective-work begin. Soon the whole campus was buzzing with Machiavellian theories. A group of literary critics is far more assiduous in unravelling clues, deciphering plots and analysing subconscious motives than any provincial constabulary. Hancock quickly established a book on the proceedings which had Nevill and Gwilliam joint-favourites at 4/1, Terry and Danny at sixes, Carstairs 7/1, Samuelson 10/1 and 15/1 bar.

'Betting's pretty brisk on you,' he confided cheerfully to Danny, inviting him to put a bet down as a hedge. 'I've taken fifteen quid already. If this carries on, I'll have to bring you in to 11/2.' Danny's fiver went on Nevill, who had mysteriously disappeared. In the ping-pong room the cock-up theory had most supporters; the old queen probably had a skinful – said Hancock – he was always as blind as a bat; easy enough for him to tip over the edge.

'There are editors I could cheerfully murder,' Gibbon announced loudly, making sure Samuelson could hear him, 'but not McWhinnie. He could be pretty snide at times, but never actually *vicious*.' Which was about as close as anybody came to paying homage to the deceased. Morris dutifully did the rounds, trying to arrange for some sort of tribute or memorial – flowers, selected readings, that sort of thing. As yet, there wasn't much enthusiasm. People were too caught up in the drama of the thing to allow themselves to contemplate such formal matters. The main result of his painstaking enquiries was to raise certain suspicions about his motivation, and Hancock decided to include him, as an outsider, at 12/1.

Carstairs did his best to distance himself as far as possible from the ensuing *brouhaha*, making it a solemn principle never to set foot in the ping-pong room (the kindergarten, he called it), which he regarded as exclusively the den of Hancock and his cronies. There was no denying the tyranny of virtue enforced by these teetotal fanatics was a little wearing on the nerves; all the same, to set up a virtual speakeasy on the premises seemed to be presuming on their hosts' sensibilities rather crudely. When he heard, from Danny, that Hancock was keeping a book on the police investigations, he firstly refused to believe it. Then he believed it only too well; it was, of course, the kind of cynical, tasteless gimmick one might have expected.

'I suppose I'm the prime suspect,' he remarked haughtily, and was more than a little dashed to find himself a mere 7/1 shot, with even Danny slated to have more homicidal tendencies than himself.

Later that evening he was composing a modest elegy to McWhinnie, in Latin hexameters – for inclusion in the next issue of *Poetry Newsletter*, in addition to, or possibly in place of his review which, in the circumstances, now seemed somewhat lacking in generosity – when there came a knocking at his door. At first, from habit, he ignored it. The knocking was repeated, softly but insistently, with an insistence he thought he recognised. He opened the door to find Powell-Davies standing there, her face pale, her clothes dishevelled, swirling all about her like loose papers on a desk. She was evidently in something of a state.

'Must speak to you,' she said. 'Can't keep it to myself. Have to tell someone and you seemed the best...'

He sat her down with what, he realised sadly, was the last of his London gin. He'd been rather hoping to hang on to that to help him through the rest of his hexameters, but said nothing of his sacrifice, and she was evidently grateful, taking it neat and knocking it back in one.

'It's Gwilliam,' she said. 'He's always been on the radical side of the Welsh Nats.' She stopped. 'No, call a spade a spade, no point in euphemisms. Not radical: sadistic. A thug. Believes in violence. Doesn't just believe in it – celebrates it – worships it. Did you ever hear his poems? No, of course not, why ever should you? Ugly Welsh rant, all about blood and fire and vengeance driving the English from our soil. He's got no end of guns – all illegal. He steals the ammunition. Luckily most of it won't fit. He can't get a licence, you see, with his record. Oh yes, he's done time, for house burnings, that kind of thing. That's when I got the divorce. If only I'd known the confounded man was here. You really should have told me, Hugo.' There were tears in her eyes and she looked, suddenly, helpless.

'What man,' said Carstairs, though he had already guessed.

'McWhinnie, of course. You should have told me. Mind you, I never thought he'd do it. He was always threatening, but I didn't really think…'

Carstairs gathered that McWhinnie was a particular *bête noire* of Gwilliam's, among a considerable number of *bêtes noires*, it should be said, and rather as a substitute for Madoc who, it went without saying, was the *noirest bête* of all.

'He always said he stole it – the poetry that is – stole it from the Welsh; and McWhinnie was there, legitimising it and making it all respectable. That's why he said he'd do it.'

'Do it?'

'Kill him. He said it dozens of times. You've no idea. He'd sit there of an evening making out lists, reciting the names, while he cleaned out his shotguns with a rag. Prince Charles, Neil Kinnock, Michael Heseltine (he hated pseudo-Welsh politicians, can't say I entirely blame him for that), McWhinnie, Cliff Morgan, Harold Evans. It used to worry me sick the way he'd find out their addresses, car registration numbers, the places they went. But I thought it was all a fantasy. I never really dreamt…' The tears rolled down her cheeks; Carstairs offered her his large white handkerchief.

'Have you told the police?'

She shook her head. 'Haven't got the nerve. You don't know what it's like, living in a place like this. The police. Most of them I used to teach, listened to their compositions, corrected their sums, smacked their bottoms and checked their dirty fingernails. It makes a difference.'

He nodded. 'All the same...'

'I know, I know. There wouldn't be any more of that gin, would there? Just a smidgeon?'

'Sorry...'

'You mean that was your last? And I took it. Oh, you are good. I'm sorry to be such a bore. I'm not usually like this...' and the tears began again.

'Gwilliam?'

Down at the station they were highly amused at the idea.

'No, no, Mrs Powell-Davies,' the inspector said. 'I'm terribly sorry but it wasn't your Gwilliam.' He sympathised with her suspicions and said they were 'very natural' in the circumstances. Speaking purely off the record, he told her, nothing would give him greater pleasure than to put that old scoundrel under lock and key for a good long time – long enough to write an epic, eh? – he said – and winked at her. Trouble was he had the perfect alibi, crafty sod. Spent the night in the police cells here, didn't he? Picked up for drunk and disorderly outside the Primitive Brethren; smashed two windows in Parry Madoc Hall and exposed himself to one of the female Brothers. You don't get a better alibi than that, do you?

'Oh God.'

'Not to worry, though. We've got the blighter that did it. Gave himself up he did. Got the gun and everything. Bit touched in the head, if you ask me.'

'But who?' Carstairs interrupted.

Strictly speaking, the inspector told him, he was not at liberty to divulge that sort of information. All he would say was he appeared to be some sort of gardener at the Hurst who had a grudge against McWhinnie. Been planning it for years.

Down in the cells Nevill was on his knees, hands clasped, praying. He'd been praying all night, lips trembling, eyes staring blankly at the slop-bucket in the corner. He wasn't praying for forgiveness, but for the strength to carry it through. He'd told them he felt no remorse for what he'd done; he'd done what he had to, that was all, and his own life didn't matter. He was willing and happy to pay whatever penalty their earthly laws decreed. All that mattered was purity and the health of the spirit. McWhinnie had been a shadow on the spirit, a dark force, impure. Now he was gone and Nevill felt free for the first time in his life, liberated; in his cell he felt, for the first time, enlarged.

Next day Carstairs received the following letter, neatly folded, in a buff envelope. It was postmarked 'Maccylynth, 4 p.m.' the previous day.

My dear Hugo,

By the time you read this, all will be known. How tawdry and disreputable it will all appear! It is to you above all, my dear friend, that this explanation is due. In all the tangled web of secrets and deceit in which I spider-like have woven and enmeshed myself over, oh, so many years, one strand above all others has caused me the greatest guilt and pain. I mean the extent to which I have entangled others, my honest friends and colleagues, in my wretched lies, traduced their trust, abused their confidence, dishonoured the very name and spirit of academic fellowship. How many times have I longed to make this confession, to set my misdeeds before you in a clear light? But to what avail? What could I say, what bond of friendship could I call on that would not merely seem to solicit acquiescence, or worse, in scholarly crimes for which there can be no forgiveness, striking as they do at the very heart of scholarship itself? You, with your impeccable instinct for all that is honest and just will not, I know, allow whatever generous sensations of compassion for a miserable sinner you may feel to obscure a proper horror (it deserves no lesser name) at the sin itself...

What I *write now is a* confessio *rather than an* apologia: *though when I use the term confession I would be understood to mean it in a legal sense only, not theological. I would not want it thought that I endeavour in any way to expiate, far less to exten-uate my crimes; merely to explain them. There is nothing that can be extenuated or excused. Yet I will say this, and you who have so often, and in so exemplary a fashion, discharged the solemn duties of an editor yourself, will best understand me; how easy, but how delusory it is for an editor to believe that everything is merely a matter of judgement; that there is no absolute right or wrong in establishing a text, merely opinion and convention. It can begin with something as innocuous as punctuation. When we modernise a comma to a semicolon, or convert a dash to a full stop, what Olympian powers we arrogate to ourselves! And what a treacherous path we embark upon! In my own case, the Madoc manuscripts with which I was entrusted were in such a fragmentary and disordered state that only the most painstaking remedial endeavours could hope to return them to any kind of intelligibility. Over many years I set myself willingly to the task of patient restoration, drafting and redrafting innumerable different decipherments of their torn and crabbed scrawl, scrupulously listing every variant, carefully noting wherever I had perhaps expanded 'ye' to 'the' or preferred a reading 'these' to 'those' or 'late' to 'fate'. Until – the inevitable result – I found myself so perplexed and overwhelmed with variants that I became increasingly unsure which was which; that is, which words were Madoc's and which my own. Still, I did not desist, but plunged on, revising where I aimed at restoration, altering where I pretended to ascertainment. In the end I fell into a kind of despair, utterly unable to determine where restoration ceased and fabrication begain. My case, I fear, is not dissimilar to that of Richard Bentley (though I would not presume to rank myself on a level with that Augustan scholar), mutilating the text of* Paradise Lost *and substituting his own tone-deaf emendations for Milton's sublime poetry. Who but the most arrogant of scholars would reject the haunting mystery of 'darkness visible' to substitute his own pedantic 'transpicuous gloom'? In recent months it has been borne in upon me, painfully, that I have worked for several years in my own transpicuous gloom; worse, that it is a gloom of my own creation and one which I have endeavoured to spread over the works of a poet I once claimed to admire. Worst of all, I have done so in the absurd belief that I was guided by the most advanced editorial principles; convincing myself, with every fresh violation of the text before me, that what I did was in the name of scholarship and enlightenment. Too late I have learnt how delusory are the claims of learning, how fragile and perishable are works of art. The breath of what we call scholarship is a contagion – it is the letter that killeth. I too have killed the thing I loved – poetry, that finest and most elusive spirit of the imagination.*

I have been contemplating for some weeks how to make atonement for my sins. At first I thought a speech, a lecture to the conference, making a clean breast of it, a confession before my peers. But in this, as in so much else, my nerve failed me. So I have resolved upon this final sacrifice. I do not in any way seek to emulate the death of Madoc himself; merely to achieve a cleaning of my troubled spirit. I, a usurper, go to seek his forgiveness, for he alone can give it. To you, my friend, I entrust the onerous and unenviable task of assuring those whose business it may be to investigate this melancholy episode, that I go to meet my fate with a mind saner and less troubled than at any time these ten years past. I can say no more.

Yours ever,
Randolph McWhinnie

Danny was woken by an insistent knocking at his door. He raised his head from the pillow. 'Come in,' he said, wiping sleep from the corners of his eyes. The knocking ceased and pushing began; but the doors locked automatically. Soon there was knocking again.

'Hang on.'

His head still ached from the whisky he'd had at the impromptu wake for McWhinnie that Hancock had organised. Any excuse for a booze-up. The lino was freezing beneath his bare feet but, just for the moment, he hadn't an idea of where his socks might be. He straightened his pyjama trousers, opened the door – and Gillian grinned at him.

'Caught you,' she said, stepping briskly in.

'Uh?'

Standing in the centre of the room, her eyes darted round, taking an instant survey. There were papers and clothes scattered here and there but, as far as

Danny knew, the clothes were all his own. Shaking his head, he did his best to clear a chair for her to sit on.

'Hard night?' she asked, plonking her canvas hold-all on the floor and lighting a cigarette. Danny should have been surprised to see her, but actually he wasn't. When his head began to clear, he rinsed his face and cleaned his teeth, and felt quite glad she'd come.

'You've made all the headlines,' she said, opening her bag and chucking a couple of newspapers on the bed. The front page photographs were identical, of McWhinnie's body floating in the pool. 'Mystery of Don's Death' was the caption. He pushed them aside.

'I could do with a coffee,' he said.

It was past eleven o'clock and the refectory was deserted, with the kitchen shutters drawn down, the tables stacked with unwashed dishes. Only the machine in the corner was working. He cadged a 20p coin and they sat at a formica table smeared with marmite and crumbs of Ryvita. The thin plastic cup was too hot to touch, and he balanced it awkwardly on the table, sipping from the brim without holding it. Gillian said she was surprised how quiet it all was. She'd anticipated lots more excitement.

'Is that why you came?'

He didn't seem overjoyed to see her, Gillian said.

'Sorry, too late. You missed all the excitement. We had that yesterday. Police, newspapers, some kids from BBC Wales. We've had our moment in the headlines. It's hardly Fleet Street out here, you know. They're not what you'd call demonstrative.' She said she'd thought he might welcome moral support. Danny stiffened. Whenever she used the word 'moral' it made him feel uneasy.

'Whatever gave you that idea?'

Evidently she was mistaken. Evidently she wasn't wanted at all.

'I didn't say that...'

'I thought you might be arrested, or anything.'

'Anything?'

'According to the papers. You do *get* papers down here?' Danny chucked his paper cup into the plastic bin. 'Oh yes,' he said, 'some of them.'

Gillian took out a double-page spread from yesterday's *Daily Mail* and spread it on the table. There were salacious accounts of midnight skinny-dipping frolics by sex-mad academics, drunken orgies... and all at this Primitive Christian college. There were several photographs, with his name and Terry's mentioned several times.

'You didn't believe all that?'

'No,' she said. 'Not all of it.'

'Oh?'

'It calls you a distinguished scholar.'

She seemed to be expecting some kind of confession from him, and it irritated him that she couldn't bring herself to mention Terry's name despite the photo of her, in a mini-skirt, looking several years younger, in the middle of the page. God knows where they'd dragged that up from. The caption read: 'Riddle of naked Prof's midnight dip'.

'It's all bollocks,' he said, as they heard the chapel bell strike twelve. 'Look, I've got to go.'

'OK.' She began folding the paper, carefully, like evidence, and placing it in her bag.

'Look...'

'What?'

'It's so difficult to explain. McWhinnie, all of it –' He shook his head.

'I see...' Her voice was brittle and cold.

'No, don't say you see, because you don't; you can't.' He felt suddenly angry.

'And whose fault is that?'

He didn't answer.

'Why d'you think I came down here?'

'You tell me.'

She stood up, zipped tight her bag, swung it over her shoulder and went to the door.

'If you want to see me, I'm staying at a pub called the Feathers or something. I'm having lunch with Hugo.'

'Hugo?'

'Like you say, it's difficult to explain.'

On the way back to his room, he spotted Hancock looking remarkably chipper for this early in the day.

'Relax old son, you're in the clear,' Hancock yelled at him across the playing-field.

'The old bugger topped himself.'

'What?'

'Off the deep end. Sent a suicide note to Carstairs.

Full confession. Fit of remorse.' Hancock strode across the field to greet him. 'Apparently the Madoc stuff's all a con. Been making it up for years. Can't say I'm surprised. I always thought there was something fishy about it. Beats me why he chucked it in, though. Could have made himself a packet.'

Danny could hardly believe what he was hearing. 'You're sure?' he said.

'Oh yeah, positive. They've had a dekko in his filing cabinet. Screeds of the stuff; odes, epics, you name it. A regular little factory. By the way, wasn't that your old lady I saw hareing off through the shrubbery? Checking up on you? I can't stand it when they start that lark. Hope she didn't catch you *in flagrante*. Don't want any more corpses on the campus. If ever you need an alibi, old sport, you only have to say the word. Good news is I took another twenty quid on you and that Gwilliam bloke last night. Naturally, I don't pay out on suicide.'

'Who bet on me?' Danny asked, but Hancock went very coy. 'Can't betray a punter, can I? Let's just say there are some people around here with a very high opinion of your Machiavellian skills. Mind you, at 13/2 you have to admit you were a very tasty bet.' Danny thanked him for the compliment, if that was what it was.

'No, wait, you haven't heard the best bit yet. You know that poofy gardener, you know the fruit 'n nutcase, what's his name, Nigel, Nevill? He keeps on insisting that he did it. They tried to let him out this morning. Told him about the suicide note and everything. So now he's pretending that's a forgery too. Refuses to leave his cell. They're carting him off to a funny farm near Cardiff. Best thing for him if you ask me. Keep him under lock and key. Even if he didn't do in McWhinnie, I wouldn't put it past him to have a go at some other poor sod. Now he's got the idea in his head. That's what they're like – do anything for a bit of attention.'

They walked back towards the Hurst, and Danny asked about the note. Hancock, never one to play down a good story, gave him chapter and verse.

'I was saying to Morris: in my opinion, I reckon that in the circs it would look pretty tasteless, to say the least, to go ahead with the Plenary Session he seems so keen on. A damn good piss-up's what we need. Give the old bugger a decent send-off. To hell with Brother Josephine. Speaking of which, did I tell you I slipped a double-vodka into her britvic orange the other night. Really perked her up. Singing sea shanties and everything. You'd never guess she was Irish now, would you? Not bad legs either. Kept saying what a delicious tang the orange had and going back for more. Funny, I've always had this fantasy about shagging a nun.'

The second letter Carstairs had received that morning was from Gillian, alerting him of her arrival. She phoned him from the station as soon as she got in to arrange a meeting – preferably somewhere discreet, she said. He heartily agreed: the discreeter the better.

He was a bit late arriving, and Gillian was already there, sipping a gin and tonic at a corner table, flicking through *New Statesman*.

'Did you tell him?' he asked anxiously, not even sitting down. Gillian shook her head.

'He seemed preoccupied,' she said.

'He's not the only one,' said Carstairs, sighing and slumping into an armchair. 'What a shambles! Why did he have to die here, of all places?'

'I don't think it was McWhinnie that was bothering him.'

'Who then?'

'I'm not sure.' She peered over the rims of her reading glasses. 'Hugo, there isn't anything I should know?'

'Know? What do you mean?'

'I think you do.'

Carstairs blushed and fidgeted with a beer mat.

'Put the case,' Gillian began, but Carstairs interrupted to say that if she didn't mind he would prefer *not* to put a case, just at the present. There were quite enough cases being put as it was. He would really rather stick to the matter itself – he avoided meeting her eyes – if she didn't mind.

Poor Hugo, how he squirmed, face bright beetroot and knees twitching up and down. Clearly there was no point pressing him further. Gillian nodded – point taken. She sipped her gin and tonic and abruptly switched tack. In the circumstances, she imagined that their little wheeze must have misfired rather badly? Not in the best possible taste? Hugo nodded. Worse than that, he said, taking out McWhinnie's letter and passing it to her. Gillian read through it quickly.

'He was right, then?'

'Who?'

'Danny. It's what he suspected.'

'He would.'

'But he was right.'

Carstairs shrugged. Right or wrong, the point was it put them in a very awkward position. It would look like a trap. As if they'd deliberately set out to expose McWhinnie; it might even seem as if they were the ones who'd driven him to – he threw up his hands. It was bloody awkward.

'Yes.'

They would have to come clean, and the sooner the better. There was nothing else for it. Otherwise people might just blame McWhinnie.

'Do they suspect?'

'Some. A Few. Less than I'd imagined. There's an American woman, Terry Franks...'

'Ah yes, the naked professor. She thinks they're forgeries?'

'On the contrary, she's convinced they're genuine. Positively pounced on them as the cornerstone of a whole new feminist theory. Insists they prove the *Basque Cantoes* were written by Jane, not Thomas Madoc.'

'Really?' Gillian couldn't help laughing.

'Naturally, when she started on her feminist high-horse, the rest got rather intimidated. She has a rather persuasive style.'

'So I gather.' Their eyes met and Hugo blushed again.

'She's sent them away for analysis. Naturally, when she finds out…'

Gillian smiled. 'I can't wait to meet her.'

11

The so-called Plenary Session was due to start at three. After various cancellations, revisions, and re-revisions of the schedule, Morris had decided to go ahead as planned, though with inevitable changes to the session programme. There were protracted negotiations with the Brethren who, much embarrassed at the publicity surrounding recent events and under strict instructions from Seattle, had at first insisted on immediate cancellation. After much argument, mainly regarding fees, they had settled for a compromise provision that had the afternoon programme beginning with a solemn and lengthy address by the Dean of Brethren. Standing at the lectern in his full purple robes, he delivered, under the guise of a funeral oration, a moralistic homily on the sins of drunkenness and fornication (which had Brother Emily nodding vigorously), the sin of intellectual pride, the crying sin of suicide and the godless anarchy of the western world which, deluded and betrayed by its so-called intellectuals, was hurtling, like the Gadarene swine, towards the abyss of Hell. After this stern and humourless performance, delivered with a fixed stare, the ranks of Brethren (who had been trooped in to stand at the back of the Hall and listen) dispersed, leaving only Brothers Josephine and Vijay sitting either side of the aisle, the one with a shorthand notepad, the other with a micro-recorder, to eavesdrop on the rest of the session and send detailed transcripts back to Seattle for scrutiny. Morris then called upon Carstairs to read out McWhinnie's last letter. Although there could have been no one in the packed Hall who had not already learnt its contents, hearing it read out in Carstairs' calm, sad, scrupulous voice cast an inevitable chill over them all. When he finished, Carstairs neatly refolded the letter and called on them all to stand for a minute's silence. That over, Carstairs begged their indulgence to say a few words in tribute and respect to the memory of his friend, their colleague, Randolph Frazier McWhinnie. Although he made no explicit reference to the sanctimonious speech of the Dean, his voice seemed full of unaccustomed emotion as he spoke of the need to resist the temptations of summary judgement and moral self-righteousness. He recounted anecdotes of McWhinnie's career in the army and at Oxford, of his bravery in the Normandy landings, and his unfailing patience as a tutor and scholar. He reminded them of Johnson's astronomer in *Rasselas* who, after a lifetime's observation of the sun, moon and planets, falls prey to the delusion that it was he alone who controlled their operation. They might do well, he said, to remember Imlac's words: 'Disorders of intellect happen much more often than superficial observers will easily believe. Perhaps, if we speak with rigorous exactness, no human mind is in its right state.' When considering the sad example of their former colleague Randolph Frazier McWhinnie, they might – rather than seizing on an opportunity for easy censure – reflect that his fate might be shared by any one of them. He paused and looked around the Hurst – at Gillian, sitting by the bust of Llewellyn the Last; at Hancock, by the door, and at Terry Franks, looking bored and impatient at the back. In this connection – he went on – he wanted to add a personal postscript, a kind of confession. He paused and took a sip of water from the tumbler before him. Stupidly, for reasons that were now of no possible consequence, and probably never had been, he had been responsible for a similar fraud. He hastened to say that when he had agreed to participate in this silly prank he had not the slightest knowledge – no, not the merest inkling of Randolph McWhinnie's forgeries; or else, he wished to make it clear, he would have had no part in anything like it. Also, he wished to have it understood that what he'd done he'd done only as a kind of game, a joke, a stupid undergraduate prank. There had never been any serious intention of dishonesty or deceit on his part. Nevertheless, in view of recent tragic events, he felt he now had no honourable alternative but to offer up his resignation as a Professor of English Literature...

There was no mistaking the sense of shock that greeted Carstairs' sudden announcement. The hall was silent at witnessing this curious tragic performance. It was the kind of last act McWhinnie himself might have dreamt of, had his courage been equal to such a theatrical moment. In her seat, her view of the platform half-obscured by Llewellyn's bust, Gillian burned with embarrassment and shame. She wanted to leap up and stop him, to exonerate him from any blame, but was unable now to move. This was his moment, and in some strange way she knew that this was the exit he had planned. Carstairs went on, his note dropped to a whisper, yet in the rapt silence it was a whisper which carried to the back of the Hall.

'To be specific,' he said, 'the manuscripts which Professor Franks discovered in the Pendower tower three days ago are not genuine. They are forgeries. They were written last week and placed in the tower, by me, in order to be discovered. I offer my sincerest apologies to Professor Franks for misleading her…'

'No!'

It was Terry, on her feet and striding towards the platform. 'They are *not* forgeries!' She brandished the file of manuscripts above her head. Carstairs tried to carry on. 'As I say, I deeply regret…' But Terry Franks jumped up onto the platform.

'They are *not* forgeries,' she yelled. 'They are quite *genyuwine*. I have proof. Here –'

She held up sheets of computer printout. 'Every known scientific test has been done upon them. The paper, the ink –'

'But that's not possible…'

'It's not only possible, it's true…'

Morris got on the platform and tried to intervene.

'Look,' he said, 'I think we ought to try to stick to the programme – what's left of it. If you'll just sit down, you'll have a chance later.'

But Terry didn't want a chance later. She refused to sit down. She insisted on her right of reply.

'I hope you're getting all this,' she said to Vijay with his micro-recorder. 'I don't know what weird game you're playing here. But I know this. What we are witnessing here is a last desperate attempt by the male academic establishment...' – Carstairs tried to interrupt her and protest, but she shouted him down – '...oh yes, the male academic establishment to suppress the work of a female genius! All this hypocritical crap about the scholarly virtues of a guy who spent his life faking it! It's sick-making. This is the club in action – the old boy's club. How appropriate to wheel in Dr Johnson, the greatest club bore of the lot! Old Randolph didn't just spend his life faking the career of some dead male hero – though that would be bad enough. It's worse than that. He did it by destroying and rubbishing the reputation of the woman who actually *wrote* the stuff!'

Despite all Gillian's prejudices – and, in the twenty-four hours since she'd read the *Daily Mail* piece on Terry Franks, she'd acquired quite a few – she couldn't resist a sudden rush of admiration for this woman's style. She had conviction. She wouldn't let them boss her about. She said what she thought and to hell with the consequences. Listening to her, Gillian was seized by an irrational feeling of elation and damn well wanted to stand up and applaud. She would have done so too, had it not been for the sight of poor old Hugo, floundering there like a wounded animal, twitching, helpless to interrupt. He stared, blinking at the folds of computer printout she had tossed across the table. It wasn't possible, he kept saying; but the more he said it, the less conviction his voice carried. He gazed helplessly in Gillian's direction; if ever he needed an ally, it was now. Poor Hugo, it was painful to watch him, stuttering and apprehensive. Of course she should help him – it was her duty. After all, the whole thing had been her idea. But, all the same, she hesitated. Much as she loved Hugo, it was more than she could bring herself to do to stand up and tell this formidably defiant woman she was wrong. Then she heard Danny's voice calling out from the back of the hall, saying that Professor Franks had not found the manuscripts alone – he had been with her (people turned to look at him) – and he had never been convinced of their authenticity. He had told Professor Franks that from the start, when she *had* believed in them. But now, from the scientific evidence – which seemed to him clear and conclusive – he wanted it put on record that he had changed his mind. He now believed it would be folly – no, worse than folly, an act of blind prejudice, not to accept these manuscripts as evidence that Jane Madoc, the sister of Thomas Madoc, had written the *Basque Cantoes*. It was the arrogant, self-righteous tone of Danny's voice which finally goaded Gillian into speaking.

She stood up nervously, her voice and limbs all shaking, trying to make herself heard in the general hubbub of people all clamouring to voice their opinions, while on the platform Morris endeavoured to maintain a semblance of order. She did not give up and, caught with something of the passionate intensity of the woman whose theory she was about to torpedo, she managed to raise her voice for long enough that gradually the other voices stilled and she was left alone.

Professor Carstairs had been most gallant in concealing the identity of his fellow conspirator – she began – but she could not sit silent and allow him to make such a selfless sacrifice. The truth was, it was she who had forged the manuscripts. The whole thing was her idea…

Once again there was total silence. Who was this woman? Carstairs closed his eyes and held his head like one in the throes of despair.

'And the evidence?' Terry said at last, her voice terse.

'I can prove it.'

There was a long humming of words. Morris beckoned her to the platform, where her throat tightened and, for a moment, she thought she was about to faint. But she took some deep breaths, steadied herself and held up her slim document wallet.

'I have the last missing stanzas of Canto VI.' She unzipped the wallet and took out several yellowed fragments of manuscript. 'If you like to compare them.' She offered them up to Terry Franks, who came forward, suspiciously, to inspect them. Morris and Carstairs peered at the fragments intently.

'But the paper, the ink, my scientific analysis…' said Terry.

'Naturally I took great care with my materials,' said Gillian. One by one they all crowded round, led first by Samuelson, who had crept back in and now stared at the tiny scrawled fragments. There was a general consent that they looked very authentic. It was beyond a doubt, said Samuelson, that it was done by the same hand as the other manuscripts, the ones that Professor Franks made such a meal of. Terry herself was in a daze.

'You say you did these yourself?'

Gillian nodded. 'I finished them yesterday.'

Morris, clinging desperately to whatever last vestiges of academic respectability these conference proceedings might pretend to, recommended the formation of a sub-committee to investigate these claims. His imagination conjured up the prospect of more tabloid headlines, a drubbing in the academic press, and the end to all his hopes of an Oxford Chair.

'I suppose you put her up to it,' Hancock whispered to Danny.

'Nothing to do with me,' said Danny, somewhat petulantly, suffering a severe blow to his *amour-propre*.

Suddenly there was a shriek from Terry.

'But they're not the same! They're different – quite different!' She waved the manuscripts of Canto VI which Gillian had brought, and which she had been inspecting carefully.

'What do you mean?' said Gillian. 'Of course they're the same…'

'I'm very sorry, but…' said Terry, placing them in front of her. 'See for yourself. The handwriting. The shape of the letters. They're *similar*, but actually quite distinct.'

Samuelson, giving them a cursory glance, agreed. The hand was slightly different, more italic, less flowing; it had quite a different character.

'But that's ridiculous!' said Gillian. 'I tell you, I wrote them all –'

'Even the spelling,' said Gibbon, suddenly spotting what struck him as a damning piece of evidence. The earlier manuscript had the word 'reliques', but here it was 'relics'. Putting them both down and peering over his spectacles, he said a contradiction like that was a bit of a giveaway. For most of the waverers that seemed to clinch it, particularly when Terry pointed out another discrepancy between a 'dropt' in the earlier manuscripts and a 'dropped' in the one that Gillian had just brought. Naturally, said Terry, she was happy to wait for a full scientific analysis before any final pronouncement. But in her own mind there could be no question about it. The two women faced each other as the others began to drift from the hall.

'Look at this "l"…' Terry began, but Gillian turned away.

'Believe what you will,' she said, 'I'm out of the game,' and, turning, moved towards the door, where Danny was waiting for her.

They buried McWhinnie on the hillside overlooking the remains of the Temple of Virtue, beside George Madoc and Abigail Pengelly, in what had once been the chapel graveyard. Getting permission for the hurried ceremony had been a perfect nightmare. Inevitably the Brethren raised all sorts of objections, and Seattle was furious at the idea. But for once Morris got his way, calmly but firmly resisting all the Dean's protests. The man had no family, and few friends apart from the handful of colleagues who had remained after the conference proper had ceased. He had devoted his life, however misguidedly, to the study of Madoc; hence where else could be more appropriate? In the end it was the thought that here, in a private ceremony in the grounds of the Hurst, he would attract less public attention and tabloid muck-raking, that had the most impact. The Dean strictly forbade any of the Brethren from taking part in the ceremony in any way.

It was a sad little group that stood round the grave in a soft, steady drizzle. Samuelson had already left for some British Council freebie in Oslo, and Carstairs was too depressed to play any part, but stood, looking on from a distance, under the trees with Powell-Davies beside him. No one had the least idea what – if any – McWhinnie's religious convictions might be, but Morris congratulated himself on managing to summon up at short notice the C. of E. (Wales) chap from the neighbouring parish to officiate. It soon became evident that the man's only reason for agreeing was to give them all the low-down on these evangelical interlopers. Evidently he had been feuding with the Brethren for years.

'Brainwashing, that's all it is. Sheer ruddy brain-washing. Worse than the ruddy Moonies,' he said, stomping through the wet grass in bright yellow wellingtons. Letters to the *Times* were needed, peti-tions, letters to MPs. He seemed under the impression that academics were people of influence.

'You know, most of these slitty-eyed kids they bring over are illegal immigrants, don't you? Make sure you mention that.' He stood on the graveside and unwrapped a paperback bible from a waterproof pink plastic bag. The people on the county council were all ruddy nincompoops, or else were on to a backhander. He wouldn't put that past them, either. Right now, what was his name? Morris told him.

'OK, here goes then. "Man that is born of woman hath but a short time to live..."'

It was left to Terry Franks, of all people, to say a few words. Confident in her new status as *the* authority on the Nightingale Group, it was a task she under-took with relish. The offer from *Shrew* had been topped by one from *Termagant*, and Rory, now her agent, was currently investigating the opportunities for a new definitive edition of Jane Madoc's *Basque Cantoes*, plus a fully researched biography. They were not merely burying a man, she declared, but an era; they were bidding adieu to an epoch in literary history.

For all his faults or, maybe even because of them, McWhinnie typified all that was best – and worst – in the old liberal tradition. His scholarly dedication became inseparable from a kind of private fantasy, a grandiose delusion, because – like so many of his generation – he had been unwilling or unable to face the challenge of reality. For him scholarship had been a refuge: he valued literature not as a reflection of reality, but as an escape route from it. How appropriate that he should die and be buried here, in a landscape so often fashioned and refashioned as a fantasy arcadia. Here nature was methodised, the poet was always a prince, and the scholar found himself elevated to an all-powerful magus reducing the randomness of events to a dream of traditional order. Carstairs, feeling the damp chill of raindrops from the overhanging branches trickling down inside his collar, gripped Powell-Davies' hand. Back in her cottage on the Aberdovey Road was a bottle of London gin, an electric fire and a snug double-bed with a deliciously lumpy mattress.

Up in his room on the fourth floor of the Parry Madoc building, Hancock noticed his clock had stopped.

'Oh shit,' he said, 'the funeral! They'll be almost finished now.' His fingers ran over the regulation grey flannel of Brother Josephine's knickers hanging across the back of a chair. There was something about their coarse puritan texture and the faint tang of disinfectant that clung to the rest of her clothing that he found strangely arousing.

'And so? What if they have? Come back here this instant,' said Brother Josephine. '*We've* only just begun.'